Author Bio

Christe Williams is a wife, mother of three and writer of erotic,

fantasy and thriller fiction novels. Her love for writing novels started in high school where she wrote many short novels in her

spare time as a hobby. Her love for writing novels grew during

her time off to care for her failing health.

This extraordinary author brings excitement, drama and sultry

fantasies to you through her relatable stories. Try not to get caught

up in the twist and turns this novel will take you on.

DEDICATION

This book is dedicated to the many housewives that struggle to find an outlet and struggle with their own identity. We all have a wild side rather we act on it or fantasize. I want to make it noticeably clear that I am not promoting infidelity in marriage. I am merely shedding light on several fantasies and stories from a housewife.

TABLE OF CONTENTS

RHIA WILD ESCAPADES

INTRODUCTION

In life we all have situations where we wish we could've made a different choice or took a different path than the one we chose. We all want to be happy and feel loved by those around us but sometimes that happiness isn't enough. What happens in life when we go searching for that love and fulfillment? Will we find what we are looking for? Will we be hurt during our search? Will we back ourselves into a dangerous corner of lust? Hell, we don't know how we will end up but we know the journey can feel so damn good. In my search to find myself and happiness that I felt I was missing I ended up losing a piece of myself and a little more than I bargained for. This rollercoaster ride felt so damn good at first until I was turned upside down. This is my life. This is my jacked-up story. This is my Ratchet tale of a housewife.

BRINGING SEXY BACK

School was back in which means I had a lot of free time on my hands in the morning. Being a housewife was not rocket science nor was it an all-day event. I have been married for 9 years and my husband and I had two kids together. My girls were my world and I loved them dearly but was so glad both were now school age. My oldest was eleven and my baby girl was five years old. My husband was an excellent provider with a good job that allowed me to stay at home. He was a police officer by day and frequently moonlighted at nights. After my last daughter I struggled to lose those extra pounds like most mothers do so with free time on my hands I decided I would join a gym.

My life was simple but rather privileged. We had nice cars, a big house in a nice area and a nice bank account to match. It seemed to outsiders that I had it all at home and did not want for nothing. But the one thing I was missing was that intimacy with my husband. Do not get me wrong we got it in when we could, and it was damn good. But it was far and few and my only other option to satisfy myself was the use of my toys. Do not get it twisted I took care of myself in that department but still there is nothing like a man and woman. I wanted and needed my husband, but he was to set on working to maintain what we had plus some. Of course, something had to fall by the waist side and that something was me. You see my husband and I had only been married for 9 years but we have been together since high school. I have always considered myself a good girl even saving myself for marriage unlike my friends.

My husband was my first and the only man I had ever been with.

I was proud to have children only by my husband and set a good

example for my girls. I just needed my husband to remember

what brought us together and made us fall madly in love. I was

starting to feel like maybe my weight or maybe even our girls

were the reason for our lack of intimacy. We have never given

each other a reason to believe we were cheating on one another

so that wasn't the issue. I believed that we just needed a little

vacation, just the two of us so that we could rekindle our love.

I remember the day my world was turned upside down. It was a

normal Friday morning, and I was up at six in the morning fixing

breakfast for my family to start their day. My husband was

getting dressed and heading into the kitchen to grab a bite to eat

before he headed into work. He had advised me the night before

that he picked up an extra shift that night and would not be home until late at night. My girls made it to the table before my husband because it was pancake day, and they loved their pancakes. My husband came downstairs, grabbed his plate that I had wrapped up, hugged and kissed us all and headed out the door. The girls soon finished up their food and I helped them get dressed to rush them to school. When I arrived back at the house, I immediately got to work on cleaning the kitchen, making up beds and prepping food for dinner. Today was the day that I decided I was going to join one of our local gyms and had an appointment with my trainer today. I wanted to get my body back like I had before my girls to show my husband I still had it and to make myself feel good. I did not know how long I would be there so I wanted to make sure I had everything prepared so once I got home with my girls, I would not have to rush to fix them dinner. I was so excited by going to the gym that I went and bought some cute little workout clothes. It did not take me long to finish my daily chores, get dressed and head out to the gym.

Now this is where my life took an unexpected turn into the danger zone. I got to the gym and filled out my paperwork for my membership and set goals for myself before being introduced to my trainer. I sat at this desk and watched several people pass me by thinking to myself my body was not as bad as my mirror made it seem. Within minutes I was approached by this tall, toned, dark skinned brother who introduced himself as Andre. My heart skipped a beat, and I began to feel those feelings I felt when my husband and I were newlyweds with no kids. He was beyond fine and I am sure my face told him that I was extremely impressed by him by the way he flashed me a smile. He looked over my paperwork for my goals and assured me that he would get my body right. Oh, my damn how I wanted him to get my body right but not the way he was being paid to. We started off our workout by stretching which involved him being a little hand on to assist me in stretching. Every time this chocolate man laid his hands on me it sent chills up my spine to a point where I was embarrassed but glad, I did not have my wedding ring on. I felt like I was cheating on my husband with my clothes still on. How can this job be legal? This man was making me wet by doing simple stretching techniques. I did not know how much more of him I could take. But I had to remain strong but the closer he got the more I could smell this brother and he smelled good. By the time we made it to the cardio area I was exhausted already from containing myself.

I was breathing hard but not from exercising. Andre was my trainer, and I did as he asked me to do and climbed on the treadmill and started with a brisk walk. I tried my best to listen to

the instructions he was given me and the breathing techniques as

he increased the speed. I could feel his eyes scanning up and

down my body as I jogged on the treadmill, but I did not mind. I

had my own fantasy going on in my mind. I soon started

imagining Andre bending me over on a weight bench and filling

me from behind. I imagined him picking me up and placing my

back against a wall as I bounced up and down his big black dick.

I also imagined us in the steam room with his face between my

thighs and his hands tightly gripping my ass. All this had me

completely zoned out as Andre stood in front of me with his lips

moving and me imagining him kissing me with those big juicy

lips and his tongue dancing in my mouth.

I quickly snapped out of my fantasy as he clapped his hands to

get my attention to end my cardio workout. I could not do

anything but blush and apologize. We then moved on to the leg area where I sat on this machine where I had to lift weights with my legs. I stayed focused on his voice for a good minute as he gave me more instructions and counted out reps for me. He told me he wanted me to feel a little burn and added some extra weight. Well, I wanted to feel more than a little burn. Sitting on that machine I could see him easily scooping my legs up as I arch my back at the warmth of his breathe between my legs. Those big juicy lips, long and strong tongue circling my clit to the rhythm of Tempo slow. I could almost feel his tongue going in and out as he moaned while ingesting me and savoring the flavor. This man had me gone in the brain thinking of what he could do to me. Hell, what I wished he would do to me, but it was all a fantasy at this point. He did a good job remaining professional during our session but that did not stop him from occasionally taking long glances at my body. Hell, to be honest I put my body in certain positions just so he could envision intimately having me his way.

As our session came to an end, he walked me over to his desk where he handed me his card while he asked me how I felt. I told him I felt good and was looking forward to our next session with a flirtatious smile. He returned the gesture and told me he would make himself available to me anytime I needed him and all I had to do was call. He took the card that he gave me, flipped it over and wrote his personal number on the card.

Now what I should have done was tell this man I was married but I could not speak those words at this point. Hell, in my mind I had already cheated on my husband and in my heart the damage was already done. I felt drawn to this man like he was a drug. If he would have asked, I would have fucked him right then and there. I felt like a teenager with her first little crush, just going for whatever came along the ride. But I was not a teenager and my situation being crucial. My body and my mouth just kept on writing checks that my ass wanted so badly to cash. I giggled like a little girl and wrote down my personal number and like a fool gave it to him. His eyebrow raised in amusement which was so fucking sexy as his bite his lip. He told me to call him after six when he got off. I smiled, turned around and walked out the gym making sure he was watching my ass.

Once I got my ass back in my truck, I could not do nothing but scream with regret, guilt and embarrassment. What the fuck had I just done and how the hell was I going to get out of this shit? I did not tell this guy I was married with children from the jump so how was I going to spring it on him now? And more importantly would he even care? The cards had been played and the challenge had been made. This man accepted the challenge when he gave me his number and took mines as well. I could feel my stomach bubble from fear. But the little lady between my legs was still throbbing and asking for more. I had to get my mind off Andre.

It was time for me to get my girls anyway, so I put on my game face and drove to my girls' school just as they were walking out together. As they got in the truck, I asked how their day was and as usual they reply in unison like twins.

My oldest asked how my day was and what did I do and Immediately my mind flew back to Andre. I gave her a generic answer that seemed to always satisfy her and drove to the house to get dinner started.

We got home right at four o'clock and it was like my mind froze

as I entered the kitchen and looked at my countertops. They were

the perfect height for Andre to place me on to have his way. Shit!

I looked around to make sure my girls were not around to

witness my body tremble in pleasure. I could not believe what

just happened to my body. I came from the thought of this man

fucking me in my husband and I home. I was riding a dangerous

line with that thought. I immediately went to my room to clean

up and change my clothes. When I returned to the kitchen my

oldest was sitting at the table doing homework and baby girl was

coloring. They both knew the drill before dinner, and I never had

to say much to them. I started dinner which was a simple chicken

alfredo pasta shells with garlic bread. Before long homework

was done and dinner was ready. We did not have to wait on my

husband because he had already informed me that it would be a late night. So, the girls and I ate, and I started running their bath water when I caught a glimpse of the clock on the wall. It was almost seven and I had not called Andre, and he had not called me. I figured maybe another woman caught his eye and he decided to try her instead. I honestly cannot say I was relieved because my body wanted this man. At the very least speak to him to see where his head was. I got my girls in and out of the tub without incident and got them both settled in their beds and returned to my room to take a nice hot bath. My body needed the soak, and a glass of wine would really set it off. I went to our mini bar and poured a glass of wine and retreated to the bathroom to add some bubbles to my bath. It was after seven and Andre still had not called or texted me. My girl downstairs was upset and obviously felt some type of way because she was still jumping for the attention. So, I returned to my bedroom to retrieve my water toy so that I could pleasure myself and then slipped into the tub with my little visitor.

I tried my hardest to control my thoughts while I pleasured myself but there was no controlling my mind nor my body. I was so bound tight at that point I just imagined that toy was Andre as I changed positions in the tub. Riding the toy, a little clitoris stimulation and even a little anal play. Oh yeah, I got myself right and the waves in the tub plus that wine made it even better as I finished up and took the fantasy to my bed. But before I could allow myself to indulge in more fantasy I checked in on my girls, who were sleep, then returned to my room. It was almost nine and I knew my husband would be home within an hour or two, so I turned my phone off. I tried my best to put myself to sleep while using the toys. I worked myself out for the second time today. I was exhausted and dehydrated by the time I was finished. I was disappointed that Andre had not called me after the time he told me to call him, but I could not dwell on that. Hell, I am a married ass woman. Eventually I rolled over and fell asleep alone as usual.

The next morning was the same as every morning. I was up early fixing breakfast for my family. My husband got home around eleven the night before but was up and already sitting at the table laughing and talking with the girls. It was an easy Saturday morning for me. My girls were spending the weekend with my husband parents and my husband was going to work. This was the day I was looking forward to, a day with my two besties. Keri was married with a son and daughter and Rae-Rae was not married but had a boyfriend of eight years and no kids. We always met up on Saturdays just to let lose for a while. I had some shit to share with them today. You see between the three of us I was the good girl, the shy one and the prude out of the group, let them hoes tell it. We all meet ten years ago in college and been stuck like glue ever since then. I must admit I was the least wild out of us three, but I was no prude. They were more experienced with men and women and even had one or two affairs before themselves. This was all new to me and I needed some advice and someone to talk me out of going down that dangerous road. Hell, them bitches would probably celebrate the news.

Well, I got my family through their breakfast and kissed my husband goodbye but not before reminding him that I would be with the girls all night. The girls were ready to go so I loaded them up and headed only ten minutes down the road to my in-law's house. I booted them girls out of the car and headed to

Rae-Rae house out in the boonies. This girl lived so far out I swear I passed Crystal Lake each time and we were in Virginia. When I arrived, they were waiting on me so I grabbed my overnight bag and headed straight to the backyard where I knew they would be. Sure, enough the heifers were already sipping mimosas and chilling on the patio without me.

Late as usual, Keri snapped. The heifer knew punctuality has never been my thing. I just winked at her as I dropped my bag and poured me a glass. I had some tea to tell my girls that just could not wait. I knew there would be no judgement amongst my girls. As I told them my tea the looks on their faces were priceless. I was not so prude to them now. Rae-Rae was the first to chime in to ask if the opportunity arise would I give into him. Honestly, I knew the answer was yes but saying it out loud was just like saying I was going to cheat with a purpose. I really wanted to see what Andre was about but did not want to compromise my marriage. Keri of course was intrigued by this mystery man and just wanted to know when they could meet him. They made it seem as if I was a single woman with a potential date. That was not my reality, more like my fantasy at this point. I explained that maybe he was leading me on because he had my number but had not called or texted me. Rae Rae took my phone and started searching for his number immediately saying she was going to text him for me. I put up some resistance, but the truth is I am glad she had some balls to do so. She then sat my phone in the middle of the table in case he responded and continued to sip on her drink. I sat back hoping he would text back so that I could hear his voice but the responsible me scolded me for even entertaining the thought. Within minutes we started discussing our plans for the minute like nothing had happened. We agreed on this new bar that recently opened. We were going to have drinks and do a little dancing and return for an adult sleep over but adult style. But before we could get too excited my phone started buzzing. I looked around the table in shock with my heart beating faster than ever. I turned the phone over to see Andre name on my screen and I dropped the phone in my lap.

My girls wanted to know what he had to say but I just wanted to get in my car and drive back into town to him. The girls urged me to communicate with him. So, while they discussed the details of our night, I tuned them out to respond to Andre.

Andre: Hi there gorgeous. I have been thinking about you. Why didn't you call me last night?

Me: I was extremely busy with my two girls yesterday and it slipped my mind.

Andre: So, you have children??? I would have never guessed. You look too young to have two kids.

Me: Well, thank you and I am young, lol.

Andre: No doubt your young baby. So where is your girls' father? Is he in the picture?

This was the conversation I was dreading having with Andre, but it needed to happen. By now the girls were standing over my shoulders invading my privacy like they always had done.

Me: Their father is my husband.

I waited what seemed like ten minutes for him to respond. Maybe that ran him off or maybe he just had to process the fact of me being married. I sat there wondering what he was thinking and how he was feeling. Then finally he responded.

Andre: Husband huh? Well, my question to you is are you happy? Does he make you happy?

Wow it seems like that did not run him off. Now this is getting real.

Me: I am content in our marriage but there is always room for improvement.

Hell yeah! I really did text that and the girls were dancing around acting crazy and cheering me on like some ghetto cheerleaders. I could tell they were buzzed off their little drinks and I felt like I needed to catch up with them.

Me: So, is that a problem for you Andre?

Andre: Hell, naw girl! I know your feeling your boy swag and I am not going to lie I am feeling you and was checking your little body out. Is that a problem? Just let me know if I am violating but I got the feeling you were feeling me too.

Me: No, you are not violating and yes you have a little swag to you, lol. I am not sure if I am feeling you or not because I do not know anything about you, but your sexy.

Andre: Ok well I am single, twenty-five with no kids. But the best way to get to know me is to hang out with me sometimes. So, when is a good time to reach out to you?

He was single with no kids but three years younger than me. I did not really mind the age difference because he was so damn fine. By this time Keri and Rae-Rae were hysterical and all for me meeting up with him tonight. What better night to hang out with him? I did not have my kids and my husband was well familiar with our girl's night and knew I was not coming home tonight.

Me: I am free in the mornings until around six most nights. Well, I am with my friend girls tonight and we were thinking about going to the new bar downtown tonight if your down to meet up tonight.?

Andre: Ok. Sound like fun but I was thinking of something a little more private and intimate if you are comfortable.

That text sent those same chills through my body that I experienced the day before. I guess he was testing me to see how badly I wanted him. The two hoes behind me were down to cover for me and did not mind me breaking our plans to chill with a new boo. Hell, for all I knew Rae-Rae and Keri had someone on the side also. I was intrigued by Andre and wanted to get closer to him so I figured I would take advantage of my freedom tonight and allow myself to be weak for once.

Me: Ok I am down to link up with just you.

Where do you want to meet up at?

Andre: Your more than welcome to come to my house if you are comfortable with that. I will even cook for you tonight.

His house? A man that will cook for me. This shit sounded too good to be true. But I could not turn him down my body had already made the decision for me. He texted me his address and we agreed to meet up at six o'clock.

The crew was beyond themselves and was discussing what I should wear. I did not bring any clothes for a romantic date, I replied. But Rae-Rae had that covered as we entered her house, she raced ahead of us up her steps to her room. I sat on the bed afraid of what she would pull out of her fuck me stash. To my

surprise she tastefully emerged with some fashionable jeans, a

cute tank top and some heels. Luckily, we were the same size

and often wore each other clothes.

We all took a few sips and agreed on the outfit then returned

downstairs.

As time went by, I could not help but watch the clock in

anticipation of seeing Andre again. My thoughts of him had been

so X-rated the day before that I started to get excited all over

again but could not let it show.

We left the house and went to a local shop to have lunch like we

did every other Saturday. Only this time I decided to eat light

because Andre was cooking for me later that night. I engaged in

conversations as much as I could, but I could not help that my mind was all over the place. I was feeling lust and guilt all at the same time thinking what if my husband were to do something like this to me. All the years we had been together I had never known him to stray. He was a hard-working man who wanted nothing more than to provide a good life for his family. I felt bad but my body was craving that attention since I was not getting it at home. It is a fact that if you neglect something too much and too long you will eventually lose it. I did not want to break up my family physically, but I felt as if my heart was up for grabs.

Once we finished eating, we walked the local shops in the area and did a little shopping before returning to Rae-Rae house. I had to prepare for my date, and they were preparing to go to the bar. I grabbed my outfit and headed to the room designated as my room for our girl's night.

There I got in the shower, got dressed and did my makeup and hair. When I came down the steps the girls were in the kitchen having pre-party shots as we called them. It was getting so close to the time I needed to head out that my nerves were rattled so I decided to take a shot also. I told them that if I felt my date was going sour, I would call them and meet up with them at the bar. They both knew better than that after all the things I told them. I agreed to keep my phone on and call them if I need them then I left the house.

MY DIRTY SECRET

On the drive to Andre house, I was excited but nervous. I knew if

I gave this man a chance, he would blow my back out and I

wanted that, I needed that. I listen to nothing but slow jams on

my way to his house to loosen up. You think that shot of liquor

would have done the trick, but I guess my nerves were worse

than I thought. I was conflicted. Stuck between what I had and

what I could possibly have. I wanted this man bad as hell, but I

did not want things to get out of hand. I figured we would meet

up when we could and do our thing and go our separate ways. A

hit it and quit it kind of relationship. The thought of him just

made me wet and I started thinking of all the things I could do to

him. My navigation said I was less than a mile away and I got

nervous all over again and started checking myself out in the mirror. As I turned on his street, I noticed how nice the neighborhood was. I did not know being a trainer was good money. I pulled in his driveway and parked beside a nice pearl colored Range Rover. Hell, this brother was doing good for himself. I texted him that I was outside and checked myself in the mirror one last time. As I added more gloss to my lips, I saw the front door open out the corner of my eye, so I took a deep breath and got out of my car.

Andre greeted me with a big smile and hugged me like we had been together before. As I entered the house I was taken back by the mouthwatering aroma and how neat and clean he was for a bachelor. I was convinced he had a female roommate, or his mom came over to clean his home. I have never met a male neat freak before it was refreshing.

Andre: Would you like a tour of my home?

Me: Of course.

Andre: We can do that after we eat. Dinner is ready and your plate is fixed. Do you prefer red or white wine?

He cooked, he fixed my plate and he had wine? Ok what is the catch? Is this man, psycho, gay, or just a hopeless romantic like I was?

Me: White will be fine thank-you. Everything looks so good.

We sat down at his table and enjoyed a wonderful meal and had an interesting conversation. We talked about our childhoods which were remarkably similar and how we basically grew up in the same area. We graduated from the same high school, but I did not know him back then. He was a breath of fresh air and I felt comfortable with him. He even told me to call him Dre so I told him instead of calling me Karhia he could call me Rhia like my friends do. He smiled and said sexy Rhea. I loved the way he said my name. We finished up at the table and he gave me a tour of his nice three- bedroom home that of course had a weight room. He took his health and body profoundly serious I could tell, and he had a nice body. Afterwards we sat in his living room grinning at one another trying to read each other's mind.

Dre: So how was your meal?

Me: It was exceptionally good. Who taught you how to cook?

Dre: (Smiling) My grandmother taught me when I stayed with her. She always said a man should know how to cook for his woman.

Me: I could not agree more she is a smart woman.

So, what is next?

Dre smiled and walked over to his stereo and turned on some

slow jams.

Dre: Next we will dance and go with the flow of whatever if that

is, ok?

Me: I like that. I can do a little something on a dance floor.

He pulled me so close to him I could smell the cologne on his

chest as we danced. The music seemed to play for hours as we

grooved from one tune to the next our bodies became more

intense. I was in heaven as his hands moved about my body.

Hell, it felt good to be admired and it had been so long since I

felt this way. It was not long before I found myself engaged in a

passionate kiss with Dre. He was the best kisser, not to forceful

but just enough to get you wet. I did not want to dance any

longer but as I was ready to stop, he fell to the couch and told me to dance for him. Dance for him? This was something new to me.

With my husband there was little fourplay that lead straight to

sex. Dre was different, but I obliged him and danced sexy for

him. He admired my body as it moved with the music.

Dre: Come here.

I could not tell this man no! I could not even play shy at this

point I was in this man's trance and ready for anything he was

willing to give. I stopped short of the couch between his legs,

and he raised my tank top just enough to kiss my belly button as

he unbuttoned my jeans. Oh shit! This is really happening right

now but still no regrets. This man had lips of velvet and the

warmest tongue. He managed to remove my jeans with no help

all while kissing and licking my stomach. I managed to grab his

shoulders as my knees became weak and he just shot me a quick grin. He stood in front of me and lifted his shirt revealing his abs

and to my surprise pierced nipples. That shit was so sexy to me. I

wanted to jump on him right then, but I held back.

Dre: Turn around.

As I turned around, I could feel him raising my tank up over my

head and my hair fell down my bare back.

Dre: Mm mm, I like that.

He just sort of stood there and admired me from the back in

nothing but my lace panties.

Dre: Turn around and let me look at you.

I turned around as asked and I could see he was ready to have

sex. The bulge in his pants was something serious at this point so

I walked up on him and started unbuckling his pants. He watched me the whole time and as his pants hit the floor, he looked me in

the eyes and grinned. But before I could say a word, he sweeps

me off my feet and carried me into his bedroom kissing my neck

the entire way. When we entered his bedroom, he returned me to

my feet, but I felt like I was still floating at this point.

Dre: Lay face down on the bed and relax.

I was so confused at this point, face down. Was that all the

fourplay I was going to get? I laid down anyway ready for

whatever surprise he had for me. I heard a drawer open, a snap

and then felt something liquid and warm pour down the crease of

my back. He then gently removed my panties and proceeded to

give me a massage. The smell of berries filled the room, and the

aroma was enticing to my senses. I laid there and enjoyed the

moment as he worked his magic. This man delivered magic with his lips and his hands so I could image what other magic he could deliver. He was spoiling the hell out of me in just this one encounter. What was his intentions? Was this man trying to make me fall for him or something? I was allowing myself to be weak for a moment but was not looking for a boo on the side. I got the feeling he was either a romantic, a player or in this for my pleasure. But I was enjoying this too much to really allow myself to become concerned.

Dre: Roll over.

I rolled over and looked him in his eyes, he leaned in to kiss me between my breast and then proceeded to pour this oil down both breasts. He gave a hell of a message and looked sexy but serious while doing so. I could feel the little hairs on my body stand up as chills ran through my body, but I was not cold. As he neared the end of the message, he slid me to the edge of the bed, and I

sat up.

Dre: Lay back and enjoy the ride.

That was easily said and done as our eyes met and he licked his

lips I knew what was in store next. He got comfortable between

my legs and put both thighs on his big shoulders with ease. I laid

back just enough to prop myself on my elbows because I did not

want to miss a minute of this man. He slowly kissed his way

from my ankles to my inner thighs where he began to draw

circles with his soft and warm tongue. He knew what he was

doing if I can say so myself.

Within seconds I could feel his tongue tracing the crease of my

thighs then the lips of my vagina. I could tell that the oil he used was edible because before I could take another breathe his tongue was moving in and out of me slowly.

I could not help but to arch my back and moan in pleasure because it felt so good, and he knew the right tempo. Hands down he was a pro at what he does, and he knew it. He gripped my ass and pulled me into his mouth, and I could feel his warm breath and it made me want to cum right then. I fought back the feeling as he used his tongue to gently stroke my clit as he still had me in his mouth. With every stroke I began to breathe even heavier than the previous stroke. What was he doing to me in that moment that made me just want to squirt so suddenly? He let out a little moan after a few minutes as I moved to the flow of his strokes. I was softly riding his face and I could tell that turned him on because he quickly got up and laid on the bed.

Dre: If you want to ride it babe you can. Come sit on my face.

I could not do anything but climb aboard with no spoken words. I was ready for the ride and must say I was enjoying every moment of it. His tongue felt so good as it slid up and down my clit, so soft and moist to the touch with an occasional suck. I could tell he was enjoying it as much as I was, but I did not want to be selfish. I was so into him at this point that I wanted to pleasure him too.

Without any warning I got up and turned to sit on his face backwards and he knew what was up. He smacked my ass, moaned and returned to his meal as I rubbed his dick through his basketball shorts. He was beyond ready for some action. He was so hard that when I reached into his shorts, he lifted his body up and pulled his shorts down without missing a stroke. He was huge! I looked in amazement wondering could I fit him into my mouth but hell I was up for the challenge. I wanted to tease him as he had done me, so I did not quickly take him into my mouth all at once. Instead, I licked up and down the shaft of his dick and could feel him tense up anticipating the warmth of my mouth. I wanted to play a little more, but he was getting so intense eating me out that I knew I was not going to last too long. I placed him in my mouth, and he let out a moan that made my body quiver from the vibrations and I knew he wanted more. I tried my best to take all his dick into my mouth but he was too big for that so I gave him all the throat I could in that moment. I was not shy when it came to sucking dick. Unlike most girls I enjoyed it and could get myself off just from giving head. No hands were my motto and I lived by it as I bobbed up and down in circles around his dick not forgetting to circle the head with my tongue. We both were so close to climax as I continued to ride his face and he was moving his hips in a thrusting motion.

He quickly smacked me on the ass.

Dre: Damn girl! Let me give you some of this dick first.

I was all for that and wanted more than ever to feel him as he slid

me down his chest. We were both breathing rather fast, but this

was like a cardio workout and I was not ready to slow my

heartbeat down as I climbed on his dick to ride him. He was big

indeed as I mounted him, I could not help but cum a little. It hurt

but felt good at the same time as I sat all the way down.

Dre: Ride this dick girl.

He did not have to tell me twice as I was already saddled up and

riding him slowly from the back. He felt so fucking good inside

of me that I had not even noticed until minutes later that he did

not have on a condom as he bounced me up and down on his

dick. Every time I opened my mouth to inquire, I could not do nothing but moan or scream out in pleasure.

Me: Damn you feel so good inside of me, fuck me harder Dre. I want you to have me like you want me.

Dre: Get on all fours them girl.

I got on my hands and knees and he entered me from the back completely filling me up. There is a fine line between pleasure and pain, and I was walking that line as he gripped my hips to guide me as he wanted me.

Me: Oh Shit!

He leaned into me and whispered into my ear while still stroking me with pleasureful force.

Dre: Take this dick girl.

I was so close to cumming again, so he started long stroking me

slowly from behind which sent me into a whirl wind of

screaming out. He could really read my body. He knew exactly

when to go slow and when to speed up. I was impressed by his

amazing technique to get me to climax frequently.

Dre: Have you had enough, babe? Do you want me to stop? Tell

me what you want girl.

Me: Do not stop I am about to cum.

Dre: Do not worry I am going to satisfy you.

And with that he swiftly flipped me over and threw both legs on

one shoulder as he elevated me and entered me from the front.

With one hand he had my legs pinned on his shoulders and the

other holding my butt off the bed as he drilled me like a solider. I

could feel every inch of him gliding in and out as I reached for a pillow. I felt like the neighbors could hear me as I screamed with pure pleasure. He was hitting that spot and I was wetter than I had ever been in my life. I could not do nothing but lay there and take the dick that I had fantasized about, and it was everything I expected and more. We both were covered in sweat but going strong as he opened my legs and delivered more slow and long strokes. I could see and feel the muscles in my stomach twitching with each stroke. What was he doing to my body and where did my body learn this from? It had never reacted like this before, but I loved every second. Dre leaned in and delivered a passionate kiss followed by lightly sucking on my neck with some breast play. I guess he wanted to show my breast some love to, so he continued his long slow strokes as he began sucking my breast one after the other. At this point I did not believe I had any fluids left in my body to give but he continued to push my body to the limit as he turned me on my side and sped up his stroke. I just held his arm as he slid in and out speeding up with every other stroke. Deeper and deeper he went until we were skin to skin and then he slowed it down but never pulled back just rocking his hips up and down in a steady motion. I could tell he was getting ready to cum because I could feel him swelling inside of me. Before I could tell him to pull out, he did just that, but it was not the finish I expected. He dropped his head between my thighs and once again began to eat me out like it would be his last time tasting me. This made me sit straight up in the bed. I had never had a man dick me down so perfectly and then eat me out directly afterwards. The swift flickering of his tongue on my clit sent chills up my spine and as I began to cum, he slid his tongue in and out, in and out until my body finished shaking. He licked his lips and flipped me over on my stomach and entered me from behind.

Dre: Are you ready to satisfy me babe?

I knew he was asking me had I had enough and was ready for him to climax. Honestly, I was well past exhaustion and needed a drink of water bad.

Me: Yes.

With that one spoken word he squeezed my ass together tightly and drilled me from behind. I could not hold back my screams at that point. The perfect curve to his dick was beating my g-spot like a drum and within minutes he pulled out and exploded on my back and ass. It was so intense for him that he screamed out also.

Dre: Damn girl. I almost did not pull out in time you feel too

good.

I was exhausted as hell, but I managed to give him a grin and a

kiss after he collapsed on the bed beside me. We were both

drenched with sweat, and mouths were dry as hell. He laid there

for a second and then grabbed my ass as he got up and went into

the kitchen for something to drink. He came back with two bottle

waters of course and quickly gulped his down and looked at me.

Dre: How do you feel gorgeous?

Me: I feel good, but you wore me out. That was a workout, and I

should be excused from our Monday session.

Dre: (Laughing) No ma'am. I want to work you out at the gym

and in my bed.

Me: Yeah, I figured you would say that. I do not know if you should be my trainer now that we have had sex. I mean you are a distraction now.

Dre: That's business of the gym and this is the business of my bedroom and your welcome to have me at both. He is such a smooth talker, and I could tell this was not going to be a one-time deal.

I had to figure some things out. But I was going to be in the moment right now and deal with everything else later.

Dre got up and headed into his bathroom and I heard the shower come on. I needed a shower. There was no way I was going to take the walk of shame out his house with a sticky ass.

Dre: Come on let us take a shower.

We took a long shower together that included some kissing and fondling. We got out and dried off and headed back to his room.

Me: Where is my clothes Dre?

Dre: Are you planning on leaving so soon? I was hoping since you had a free night that we make the most of it. I figured you could stay tonight, and I would get up in the morning, make you breakfast and then you could head back to your friends. I could not believe what I was hearing. I guess he was trying to see if I wanted more than a one-night stand. But could I keep this relationship up?

Me: If you insist on me staying, I would be ok with that but only if, you are sure. I am ok to drive.

Dre: Ok, let me rephrase. I would like for you to stay the night.

And just like that I was spending the night with Dre. I went to the living room to get my phone to text my friends, but I already had several text messages from them.

(Reading messages)

Well, we know you had a good night hoe! Have fun and we will see you in the morning. Be ready to dish out all the tea!

Kisses!

I returned to the bedroom with my phone and climbed in the bed with Dre. We made small talk and cracked a few jokes before he wrapped his body around me, and we fell asleep.

DON'T CALL ME A SLUT

We got up rather later than planned but Dre cooked me breakfast as he promised. I must admit it was nice to have a man cater to me for once. And do not let me get started on the mind-blowing sex that he delivered. You would think this man was a gift straight from God himself. He was single, no kids, had his own place, job security, could cook and his sex was on point. I hit the jackpot, but he could not fully be mines I was married.

I finished my meal and said my goodbyes though I would see him tomorrow for our gym session. I got in my car for the ride back to my friends who I knew were waiting to hear about my night with my mystery guy. It was almost noon, so I already knew what they were doing and like clockwork when I pulled in the driveway they came from the backyard with glasses in hand.

Rae-Rae: How did it go, slut? I know it went well because you are

here rather late.

Keri: Yeah, how did it go? I cannot believe you went over there

and stayed the night. Kudos! You have more balls than I do. I

would be scared my husband would find out.

Rae-Rae: That is because your too emotional to cheat on your

raggedy husband. Guilt would eat your little ass alive. Me on the

other hand, fuck it I am going to live my life to the fullest.

Me: You two raggedy bitches can wait until I get fully in the

house and I will have a tell all session. Let me get out the car and

get me a drink too, damn!

I finally got out my car and sat comfortably on the couch with

my drink and these heifers were looking at me like they were

dangling from a cliff. I could not do nothing but laugh and

finally started telling them about my night with Dre. I could tell

by the silence and their faces they were just as impressed with

Dre as I was. He was a hell of a man and nothing like the men in

our lives.

Keri: Bitch, no you did not give it up on your first little date!

Rae-Rae: That is my girl! Live your life! Does he have a brother

or sister like him?

Keri was a little more reserved than Rae-Rae and I. She messed

up in the past in her marriage but vowed never to do it again. I

always felt if she did, she would not tell us about it. Rae-Rae on

the other hand was the wild child. She was into whatever made

her feel good, men or women. I guess that is why she was not

into settling down. I could not blame her either. I felt like I

settled for a provider at times instead of a compatible

companion. But I still loved my family I just wished my husband would try more.

Keri: So, are y'all going to continue to see each other? You cannot go back to that gym and if you do you need a new trainer.

Me: Of course, we will see each other when we can. And I will keep him as my trainer. Hell, he is eye candy and motivation.

Keri: Girl that shit sounds dangerous. He wanted you to stay the night, it sounds like he is into you.

Rae-Rae: Shit, I say go for it! This man could change your situation for the better and sounds like you could possibly be happy. You just have to play the field.

Keri: But that could also put you in a position where you would possibly have to give someone up. You cannot have the best of both worlds.

Both of my friends were right. It felt good at this point and I did not want to get off this ride. But on the other hand, it could get a little crowded and I must make a choice. It was too early in the game to make drastic decisions. Afterall, this was just one night, right? Dre might find someone else at some point and move on. I did not want to allow myself to stress thinking about it.

Me: We just having a little fun with each other. It is nothing serious and we both know that.

Keri: I hope not. I would hate to see you hurt.

Rae-Rae: Girl, live your best life. If that man is making you happy in this moment keep it going.

Therefore, it is sometimes good not to tell your friends everything and keep shit to yourself. Some will have you worried to death while the others will egg you on into some bullshit. I quickly changed the subject so shit would not be all focused on my black ass. I was starting to feel a little heat coming from Keri.

Me: So how was that new bar?

Rae-Rae: It was the bomb girl and packed with people. The food was ok but them drinks were on point! Mrs. Tight-ass over there was somewhat of a buzz kill so I missed my other wild child.

Keri: Girl bye I was not a buzz kill I was just trying to keep you from doing something crazy as usual. I cannot help that I must play mom when we all go out.

Me: (Laughing) Keri couldn't've been that bad?

Rae-Rae: Shit! I had this one fine ass brother that was laying drinks on us left and right and she was anti-social towards him and his friends.

They even wanted to sit with us.

Keri: What I look like surrounded by a bunch of men if my husband would have popped up?

Rae-Rae: That ugly ass negro is not popping up anywhere but in a nightmare!

Keri: Rude! My husband is not ugly. He is just not your cup of tea which is a shocker being that you will sip from different styles of mugs.

Rae-Rae: Do not make this about my sexual preference. Truth be told you need a chick to turn you out one time. Maybe then you could open your eyes to the free life.

Me: You hoes are crazy. I am glad to hear that y'all did and did not have fun all at the same time. That just means that I am not as square as you make me seem.

Rae-Rae: Yeah, it was fun but would have been better if my partner in crime would have been there to save me from the law, sitting right there.

Keri: Rae-Rae you are a psycho. Anyway, are we going to go have lunch before we all go our separate ways and back to our Monday to Friday lives?

Me: Yes, let us hit the Sandwich shop.

Rae-Rae: Sandwich shop? Bitch we are hitting the Butchers shop.

Keri: Yes, steak is my vote.

Me: Fine but I am eating lite because I need to watch my figure.

Rae-Rae: Do not worry Mr. Andre will watch your figure for you.

Me: Shut the whole in your face. Let us go because I must pick the girls up soon.

Just like that we were in our individual vehicles headed to our destination. Luckily for me it was not too far from my in-law's house. We had a nice meal together and set up our plans for our next get together and went our separate ways.

On the drive to get my girls Dre texted me to tell me he had a wonderful time with me and was looking forward to our next encounter. I returned a text letting him know that I felt the same and that I was on my way to get my girls and head home. I told him if he did not hear from me tonight, I would see him in the morning for our workout session. Just a text from him made me have a few flashbacks while driving. The way he kissed me and looked me in my eyes while we were intimate was so sexy. I knew what I was doing was wrong but for some reason I just could not help myself and partially did not care. I knew I did not want to break up my family, but I also knew I did not want to

end whatever he and I had prematurely.

I arrived in a timely manner and got my girls and insisted to my

in-laws that I was not coming in to visit. They were nice and all,

but I have always had the feeling that they never really liked me.

I never really visited unless my husband was with me. I waved

and the girls came sprinting out of the house, hugged their

grandparents and raced to the car.

Me: Hi babies, how was your weekend?

Reign: It was good mom we had a lot of fun. Grandma said we

could come over this weekend if we wanted to.

Raeleigh: Yea ma can we come back to pop pop house. Reign has

to go to real school. I am in baby school I can stay at pop pop

house.

Me: We will see about this weekend cause your dad might take off. And Rae you are not at a baby school it is kindergarten and just as important sweetie.

Raeleigh: Ok ma but I still want to stay next week.

I love my two girls and could not imagine my life without them. They were two little women with a lot of personality. My oldest Reign was very independent, smart and loved reading. She was my little professor. That baby girl Raeleigh, she was a ball of energy that rarely sat still. It is hard to say what she liked and did not because she was always all over the place. I do know sitting still is a definite do not like.

I finally got the girls home and to my surprise my husband was home, and I could see smoke clouds coming from the backyard, so I knew he was barbequing.

Girls: Dad's home!

They jumped out the car and ran right through the backyard gate.

It was not like my husband to be home so early in the day. So, I

got out the car, grabbed my bag and followed behind the girls.

Kevin: Look at my three favorite girls!

Girls: Hi dad!

Me: Hey honey. Why are you home so early?

Kevin: I just wanted to do something special for my girls. How

was your weekend with the crew?

Now normally I would have something crazy to tell him, but I

really did not want to discuss my weekend with him.

Me: Same as always there is a beginning, middle and end. We

have a blast every time we are together.

Kevin: Dig that. And how was my angels' weekend with the grandparents?

Reign: We had fun dad.

Raeleigh: I am going back next weekend dad.

Kevin: Oh, now? Don't you want to spend time with me this weekend?

Girls: You are always working, dad.

Kevin: Well, this weekend is dedicated to my girls. Whatever y'all want to do we will do. I cleaned the pool so you can go put on your bathing suits and hop in for a while.

Girls: YEAH!

Me: So, you are not working this weekend? Is everything ok at work?

Kevin: No, and everything is fine. I feel like I have been

neglecting my girls lately so I told my Sergeant that I would not

be working today or this weekend.

Me: Oh ok.

Kevin: You do not sound like you want me home? Do you have

other plans for the weekend?

Me: No, I am just a little shocked. I am happy to see you and

spend time with you since your rarely home.

Kevin: Yeah, the past two months have been crazy, but this

quality time is long overdue. Plus, maybe we can get started on

making that son I want.

Kevin loved our girls, but he has expressed several times that he

wanted to try a third time for a son. Every man wants that little

boy.

Me: Oh, now? Another baby? Are you sure you can handle me and another pregnancy?

Kevin: (Laughing) The pregnant you is something else but I can handle you and much more for a boy. Why don't you go put your bag up and make a salad the meat is almost ready?

Me: Ok.

It is funny how suddenly, my husband wants to be home more often. Could he sense something was up? And what was all this baby talk suddenly? We had not had this discussion since Raeleigh was two. I started to get a little nervous with the thought of me possibly getting pregnant. The thought had never crossed my mind with Dre. I was on birth control and my husband knew this, but Dre did not, and I must admit our sexual encounter was not at all protected.

I returned outside with a side dish for his barbeque within minutes the girls were busy in the pool and Kevin was sitting near the grill.

Kevin: So, what do you say?

Me: Say about what?

Kevin: (Laughing) Us giving it one more try and have another baby? I know you are on birth control so you would have to get off that asap.

Me: Do you really think this is a good time? Your always so busy at work and I have my hands full with the girls.

Kevin: Baby your stronger than you give yourself credit for. I know you can handle it. Plus, I will do all I can do to be here for you and the new baby. I will cut back on my hours.

I could not tell my husband no. I knew he wanted another child, and nothing would make him happier. I wanted to make him happy but the thought of Dre complicated things. I was having strong feelings for him and could still feel his touch. That man made me want to change my current situation and another baby would just add to the chaos. I still could not fix my lips to tell Kevin no.

Me: I will make you a deal, I will stop taking the pill and we will see what happens.

Kevin: Great! I would love to start practicing for that boy tonight.

Me: I know you would.

It took us a while to get pregnant with both our girls so in the back of my mind I had time. I knew Dre and I would have to be more careful or just end the little fling we had going on. Oh, but that man made my body tremble at just the thought of him. I must be with him again. This was not going to be a spare of the moment fling. I loved my husband but somehow, I felt like I loved Dre more. He was giving me everything that my husband was not and could not give me. I felt like a slut. How can I possibly love two men?

Kevin soon finished dinner and urged the girls to come eat. We sat down on the patio and have a nice dinner, just the four of us and the mystery guy in my mind.

That night I made love to my husband as he wanted but it was nothing like the night before.

He tried and gave it his best effort to break me down, but my body did not feel the same. I still made him feel like a man and as he fell fast asleep, I rolled over and silently cried myself to

sleep as I did most nights.

SORRY NOT SORRY

The next morning, I felt horrible about the night before as I

cooked my family breakfast to start their day. I was literally

making love to my husband while thinking about Dre. That man

really got into my head and having sex with my own husband felt

foreign or like a chore.

Raeleigh: Mommy can daddy take us to school today?

Me: That is up to your daddy, baby.

Kevin: Sure, I will princess, finish eating.

Reign: Cool we get to ride in the monster truck instead of moms'

little truck. Can you pick us up also?

Kevin: (Laughing) Your mother has a SUV and I think I could manage to get you two angels from school today.

Girls: Yeah!

Me: (Whispering) Are you sure you can handle that with your schedule? I am going to the gym, but I do not have much planned today.

Kevin: Babe, I got this. I want to show you that I am serious about adding on to our family.

Reign: No dad! No more babies! Raeleigh is more than enough plus she will not stay out of my room.

Raeleigh: I do not go in her room much daddy.

I want a little baby sister to play with!

Kevin: Mommy and I are working towards adding another special angel.

Reign: Aw, man!

Raeleigh: Yeah!

Me: Do not get the kids too hyped up about this Kevin it could take some time.

Kevin: I know babe, I am just so excited. Come on girls let us get ready to head out.

Once Kevin and the girls headed out, I could not help but feel guilty about my love affair with Dre. I knew I had a session with him and would have to confront my demon. I really did love my husband and had no intentions of leaving him but

Dre possessed all the qualities that I needed Kevin to have. I was torn between the two in a way and I knew in my mind I needed to break it off with Dre. So, as I did every day I cleaned up after my family and prepared for the gym. I was dreading having that conversation with Dre, but I could not expand my family and continue an affair with Dre.

Once I arrived at the gym my anticipation of seeing Dre intensified and my feelings began to shift. I was excited to see him, talk to him and touch him. I walked into the gym with the sexiest walk I could muster up just to draw attention to my ass. I wanted to draw him in and get his attention. I was a little early, so I started stretching to prepare for my workout. As I rose to my feet there stood Dre looking sexier than ever with grey sweatpants on and a tank that partially exposed one pierced nipple. Oh, how I wanted to just jump on him right then not caring who would see us.

Dre: Good morning, I see your ready to begin today.

Me: Yes, I am. Where are we starting today?

Dre: Today we will warm up with cardio and move straight to weights.

He was all about business today and kept it very professional, but I could always catch him giving me that look of enjoyment as I jogged on the treadmill. As my warmup came to an end, he urged me to get some water and head to the weights where he would be. I did as I was told and quickly made my way to the weight area where he had several different weights lined up for me. I wanted so badly for him to come out of character just for a second to let me know he was thinking of me the way I was thinking of him, but he stayed in character. Dre began to show me the many different exercises he wanted me to perform, and I moved in closer to him and grazed his leg with the tips of my fingers discreetly. He let off a little smile and shot me a sexy

gesture. He knew I wanted a little more attention. I got into

position for the first set of exercises, and he came up behind me

and grabbed my arms to help guide them correctly. I slowly and

discreetly moved my ass back into his crotch just as he let out a

low grunt. I could tell he liked it as much as I did. He leaned in

to whisper in my ear. Dre: Do you know what you are doing?

Me: I do, and I know you know what I am doing.

Dre: Do you want me?

Me: Yes.

Dre: Do you want me here?

The thought of having sex with him in the gym excited me and sent

my adrenaline into overdrive and my body became hot. My

breathing became heavy, and he could tell the question turned me

on and he knew the answer.

Me: Yes, I do. I want you right here right now.

Dre: What if I say you can have me now, would you be down for

it?

Me: Yes.

He slowly grabbed the weights from my hand and placed all the

weights back into their place. The gym was not crowded with

people on this day, and I could think of several places we could

have privacy. I was ready for whatever Dre wanted to do.

Dre: Follow me.

Me: Ok.

I followed Dre down this hall that included tanning rooms, sauna and steam room. We came to a room labeled massage room and my heart sped up. He turned and looked at me with a sexy smirk as he opened the door and we entered. He closed and locked the door behind us and there was a curtain in front of us he moved aside. I could see several different massage tables, a small hot tub and private steam room. This must have been a personal massage room for exclusive services.

Dre: Are you sure this is what you want?

I wanted nothing more but to answer him but instead I removed my shoes, top and spandex shorts. He stood there admiring me in my bra and panties and then moved closer to me.

Dre: Damn girl you are so beautiful.

He grabbed my hand and pulled me into him for a passionate kiss as he slowly ran him fingers up and down my back. I let out a little moan as he unsnapped my bra and let it fall to the floor. I wanted this man so bad that I did not care if anyone walked in or even could hear us. All I knew in that moment was I wanted him deep inside of me. I kissed him back as I ran my fingers along his sweatpants feeling every inch of him. He was ready with no assistance from me and that turned me on even more. He took his shirt off and then dropped his sweats and boxers to the floor and guided me to a massage chair. He removed my panties slowly as he kissed up and down my thighs and then gently pushed me back into the chair. Without wasting a second, he dropped to the floor and started kissing up my legs as he turned on the chair to vibrate. It felt good but I knew his tongue would feel even better. As I laid back to enjoy, he pushed my legs back as far as they could go and slowly started licking me up and down moving to the rising and falling of my chest. He went around and round with his tongue until he finally inserted his tongue inside of me slowly delivering a flickering motion inside of me like he was eating an ice cream cone. It felt so good I put my hands on his head and urged him to fuck me with his tongue. He loved it when I grabbed his head because he let out a growl and began moving in and out even faster. This made my toes curl, and my eyes roll to the back of my head. He had me and he knew it. He replaced his tongue with two fingers and immediately went for my clit that was sitting there waiting for her turn. His fingers became wet as I began to cum with the sweet soft flicker of his tongue, but he was not going to let that be the end of my pleasure. He was not done with me that easily. He continued fingering me moving faster and deeper than before. His tongue flipped and moved faster across my clit as he shook his head like a dog with a bone. Shit, it felt so good I could not control my body and within minutes I had come back-to-back and that made him happy as he sat up and licked his fingers and lips. I decided to lean in and enjoy the flavor of the day with him. He grabbed my hand and guided me on top of him on the floor where we continued our passionate kiss as his manhood throbbed between my legs begging for attention. I wanted nothing more but to take him into my mouth until he was satisfied but he had other plans in store. Obviously, this was not about him but instead all about me. We got up from the floor and I followed him into the steam room as he cut it on.

He laid a towel out on the first bench and sat down on it. He grabbed my hand and pulled me between his legs.

Dre: Turn around and ride this dick from the back.

I did as I was asked and slowly lowered myself into position on top of him. I could not help but let out a rather loud moan as I sat all the way down on his dick. He was so big and erect just on insertion I came a little. He made sure to straddle my legs on him so he could control me. I loved when he controlled my body because he seemed to know exactly what I wanted. I loved being handled and controlled and he was good at that. I could not help but lean back onto him as he bounced me up and down on his dick switching up his stroke intensively. I watched his dick appear and disappear in the glass of the door before it completely fogged over, and we were fucking in a cloud of steam. By now he had buried his nails in my hips as he grind me on top of him and he was hitting my spot causing me to cry out in pleasure.

Me: Fuck me Dre. Fuck me harder. Do not go easy on me this time. I can handle it.

At that time, it felt like the right thing to say but I soon

discovered that I had awaken a beast within Dre and he swiftly

stood me up and bent me over the bench.

Dre: Are you sure you are ready for that and here?

Me: Yes daddy.

He grabbed the back of my neck and pulled me onto his dick.

Dre: And you do not care if someone hears you?

Me: (Grunting) No! Fuck me!

Dre: Say no more.

When I tell you, this man has the magic stick, I am not lying he

had my body paralyzed. I took all ten inches of this man as he

rammed me from the back. He pulled my ponytail and rode this

ass like we were in a Kentucky Derby and that turned me on so.

My legs could not stop trembling and buckling and that made

him want to go even harder. He made me get on all fours to give

my legs a break but that did not matter one bit. With each power

stroke he strokes a nerve in my body, and I bit my lip until it bled

trying not to scream out. I could not hold it back. I enjoyed it all

and I began to scream as my body released a stream of fluids that

ran like water down my thighs. This made Dre throb and thrust

even more as he delivered long swift strokes and smacked my

ass. I was trembling but managed to cry out in pleasure.

Me: You feel so damn good.

Dre: Do you want more?

Me: Please.

Dre: Turn over.

I turned over and before I could position myself, he had cuffed my legs and picked me up. He placed his back against the wall and began giving me all of him. My legs were on his shoulders and he had pinned my thighs together as he tightly gripped my hips and was roughly bouncing me up and down. I knew I could not handle this angle too long because of the angle of his penetration. I could feel him in my ass as if we were doing anal. In this position my orgasms were stronger than ever, and he could see tears leave my eyes as I came so he placed me on the top bench and mounted me from the back. As he started delivering the dick again, he grabbed my neck and kissed me.

Dre: Am I hurting you babe?

I could not answer him, so I just shook my head because I did not want him to stop.

Dre: Do you want to do something a little different?

Me: What do you want to try?

I could almost guess he was asking me about anal sex. Do not get

me wrong I like anal sex, but I knew we would have to slow our

pace with that.

Dre: Do you want to do anal for a minute?

Me: You know you cannot be as rough, but I am all for it.

I think we got caught up in the moment and somehow forgot

where we were. Before long we were going strong again and he

had placed his finger in my butt which really turned me on. I

could tell he was ready to cum because before I knew it, he had

pulled out and slowly began entering me anal. I was glad I was

on my back with my legs up because I could relax more as I

slowly guided him all the way inside of me. He really enjoyed

the feel of my ass.

Dre: Mm mm, shit girl! Damn this shit feels so damn good. I

cannot hold out too much longer.

And with those words I sat up and grabbed his neck to pull up

and slowly grinded on his dick until we both came.

Dre: (Laughing) Damn girl I am speechless.

You see what you do to me?

Me: No, the question is do you see how you do me? We are in

your gym having sex like some teenagers.

Dre: Shit! I forgot where the hell we were. I am so sorry babe, but

I got to get up out of here before they come looking for me. Hell, I

hope they have not already.

Me: Ok do not worry about me. I am going to clean off and I will

be out behind you. I will text you later ok.

Dre: Ok.

I could tell Dre had forgot where the hell we were. He seemed

turned around as we exited the steam room to wipe off and put

our clothes back on. He did all this within three minutes, blew

me a kiss and swiftly exited the room. I could not do nothing but

sit there for a minute after putting on my clothes. It suddenly

dawned on me the conversation I was supposed to have with Dre.

I was stunned that I was that damn weak for him. I was in a

whole lot of trouble and knew there was only one levelheaded

person I could talk to about this.

Me: I have got to call Keri. I need some serious help.

I walked to the door and tried to pull it together the best I could and exited the room and swiftly exited the gym without making one stop.

Once in my truck I just sat there staring in my mirror at myself. How could I on one hand agree with my husband on expanding our family and on the other hand continue this risky affair. We just had another freaky encounter without protection, and I was no longer taking my pills. My husband made sure of that by flushing them days before. I was really asking for trouble and needed to get my head on straight. I knew Keri would be home, so I texted her to meet up with me at my favorite sandwich shop. Within minutes she agreed and said she would see me in fifteen minutes. I knew my drive would take that long, so I pulled out of the parking lot and headed to my next destination in shock.

IS THERE A PREACHER IN THE HOUSE?

As I pulled into the parking lot, I could see Keri sitting in her car smiling and waving. I tried to give a fake smile, but I was in my feelings.

Keri: Hey there girl! Free time on your hands I see.

Me: Girl. We need to have a serious talk and I do not know where to start.

Keri: What is wrong now?

We walked into the shop and ordered our normal sandwiches and sat at our favorite table away from a crowd. I took one bite out of my turkey club on rye and began to speak.

Me: I tried to break it off with Dre. I went to the gym with the intentions of telling him I could not continue this thing we have but somewhere I went wrong. Next thing I knew we were having sex at the gym. Not just sex but we were really lost in each other. I do not know what to do. I am drawn to this man in the most mysterious way.

I could tell Keri was stunned by my words because of the expression on her face.

Keri: In the gym! Are you crazy? Are you trying to get caught? It is bad enough you are cheating on your husband but to do it out in the open is past risky.

Me: Trust me I feel bad. Kevin and I are trying for another baby and I know I need to end this affair but when I am around him I cannot. we have not been together long, but I have a connection with Dre. He fills the void that I have in my marriage perfectly. He is everything I want Kevin to be and more.

Keri: Girl, will you listen to yourself? I cannot with you right now. You need to leave this man alone. It was fun in the beginning just to fool around but now you sound like you are in a relationship on the side. To me it sounds like you are his jump off.

She was completely right I was in over my head with Dre. I needed to end it with him so that I could make things right with my husband.

Me: I need a preacher, some prayer and a possible miracle. I have to stop going to that gym and separate myself from Dre.

Keri: That is the smartest thing I have heard you say. Maybe you should go talk to someone.

Me: I cannot talk to no one about this! I do not want to break up

my marriage.

Keri: No someone like a preacher or a therapist because you need

some help with this situation. You can always confide in us as

your friends, but we are not professionals, and this is your life we

are talking about.

Me: Yeah, your right I need to take this seriously before it gets out

of my control.

Keri: Good, glad we had that conversation now

I must jet. I promised my daughter I would have lunch with her at

school today. Call me later if you need me.

Me: Ok, have fun.

Keri was once again right I needed to get control of this situation

before it was out of my control. If I needed to seek professional help, then that is what needed to happen. I sat there and finished my meal playing chess in my head trying to figure out my next move. I know I needed to go home to clean up because I could still smell Dre on me and my clothes. The scent of him on me further seemed to complicate the situation. As soon as I was finished, I rushed home to get cleaned up.

When I pulled into my driveway, I could see that Kevin's cruiser was in the driveway. What the hell was he doing home, and I hope nothing is wrong. My mind was all over the place as any policeman spouse would be. I was not even concerned with Dre at this point. I rushed into the house with no hesitation.

Me: Kevin!

Kevin: Yes, babe I am here in the kitchen fixing me a snack.

Me: Is everything ok?

It was not like Kevin to come home much in the middle of a shift. But ever since the baby talk, he would occasionally speak of coming home for an afternoon delight.

Kevin: I just wanted a sandwich and possibly a taste of your snack if you know what I mean.

Are you just getting home from the gym?

Me: No, I met up with Keri for a second before coming home. Let me go jump in the shower I am not at all decent for any afternoon snack.

Kevin: No worries babe I am getting ready to run out anyway to finish this shift. I just wanted to drop in on my favorite girl.

Me: Ok, we will be safe, and I will see you later.

Are you getting the girls, or should I?

Kevin: I can manage to get them.

Kevin kissed me and headed out the door and I could not do anything but stand there in a state of shock. I had just slept with Dre and then I come home to my husband who had the intentions of sleeping with me. This was way too much for me to keep up with. I do not see how people can lead double lives or multiple relationships and not go crazy. I did not want to dwell on it, so I started a load of clothes and got in the shower. Relaxation time was over, and it was time for me to start to prepare dinner for my family and do a few house chores.

It was not long before Kevin and the girls were pulling in and dinner was finished just at that moment.

Reign: Hey mommy!

Raeleigh: Hi mom.

Kevin: It smells good in here babe and I am starving.

Me: You three get washed up and come to the table because dinner is ready.

I managed to feed my family, help with homework, clean up and get the girls in the tub and bed in record time. I was proud of myself as I entered my room to Kevin laid across the bed waiting on me. I knew what that meant just as any married woman. We spent the night entangled in several positions until we eventually fell asleep in each other's arms.

A few weeks went by and my marriage was at an all-time high with this baby making plan in place. Kevin was home more and given me all the attention I could handle. My girls were nearing the end of the school year and doing very well.

As for Dre and I we were still occasionally seeing each other but not as often because I stopped going to the gym. I was slowly breaking away from him for the sake of my family. I must admit I had one or two weak moments where we were sexually involved but I was doing better mentally dealing with him.

My marriage was almost picture perfect as I sat at my countertop looking at several vacation destinations for the summer. Kevin suggested that we take a trip for the summer before we become pregnant and bring in another member of the family. We would have all weekend to pick and map out our vacation because I was not meeting up with the girls this weekend. Keri was out of town for an in-law's funeral and Rae-Rae was away on a four-day conference with her job. I was finally happy and content with everything around me for the first time in years and it seemed as if my luck was turning around.

As I sipped my juice and thumbed through the vacation brochure a text came through from Kevin letting me know he was thinking about me and was not able to make it home for lunch. I was looking forward to our little romantic quickie, but I understood he was busy. I had not heard from Dre in a couple of days and was not really worried about that. I assumed he had met someone else and was going on with his life as I was. I decided to grab me a snack and head to the living room to watch a little television since Kevin was not coming home anytime soon. I really had not had much of an appetite the past few days but for some odd reason I wanted some hot wings and cheese squares. It was an odd combination but hey that is what I wanted. I knew those things were not here in the house, so I had to get out for food. I jumped up and got dressed while I ordered some wings from a spot near my house. I might as well have wings for dinner also. My family will be shocked by me not cooking because it was not often that we ordered in.

I jumped in my car and drove to a corner deli for my cheese

before I picked up the hot wings and quickly sped back home to

enjoy myself before my family were expected home. I could eat

and watch television in peace without any interruptions or weird

looks at the combination. I ran back in the house and flopped

down on the couch and ate twelve wings and a fist full of cheese

and it surely hit the spot. Before I knew it, I had dozed off right

in front of the tv.

I was awoken hours later by the chime of the front door opening

and in ran my rowdy girls headed my way.

Reign: I smell hot wings! Can I have some?

Me: Hello to you too child. Go to the table and start on your

homework and I will warm you up some food.

Raeleigh: Did you get chicken fingers mom? I like chicken

fingers.

Me: Hello to you too little woman and yes, I got you some

chicken fingers. Do you have any homework?

Raeleigh: No mama I just have to practice my name.

Me: Well, go to the table and get started I will warm your plate up

also.

Kevin: Hey there beautiful. You must have had a nice relaxing

day because you are glowing.

Me: My day was the same as usual, but I did have a nice

refreshing nap before you got here. I hate we could not keep our

afternoon appointment.

Kevin: Yeah, it was a lot going on today. I see you got a head start

on looking at vacation spots.

Me: Yeah, I looked over and highlighted a few places. Go get

cleaned up and I will fix your plate.

I placed the girls at the countertop to eat while they did their

homework and Kevin, and I went to the living room to eat and

discuss our family trip. We had not really said anything to the

girls about it, so we wanted to surprise them.

Kevin: I would not mind going somewhere that has a beach. The

girls love to swim, and we have never taken them to a beach

before.

Me: That is true it would be nice. Do we want to do something

local, Florida or should we do something like Hawaii?

Kevin: Hawaii sounds nice but that sounds awfully expensive and

with us planning for another baby I was thinking more like

Florida.

We can take them to the theme parks also.

Me: I never thought about that. Florida it is. I know the girls will be excited about that trip.

The girls soon finished up in the kitchen and went to take their baths and get into their bed clothes. Afterwards we sat up for a minute and had a little family time playing Uno which was rare, but we were getting better at times like these. I started feeling a little sick to my stomach. I guess I overdid it on the hot wings because I started to get lightheaded.

Me: Babe I need to lay down because I am suddenly not feeling too well. I think I may have eaten too many wings tonight.

Kevin: Go lay down babe and do not worry about the kids I will put them to bed soon.

Girls: Good night, mom.

I went back to my room to lay down but before I could lay down, I had the overwhelming urge to throw up and sprinted to the bathroom. It seemed like I was in there for hours and had threw up everything I ate as I stared at the colors of wings and cheese in the toilet.

Me: Damn that was intense.

I had never in my life threw up so violently. I guess my choice of food tonight had gotten the best of me. Hot wings and cheese taste like heaven going down but felt like hell coming back up. I immediately brushed my teeth and took some Pepto to settle my stomach and went to lay down.

I must have been out of it the next morning because by the time I woke up my house was empty. Kevin had got the girls up and taken them to school before work. The minute my feet hit the

floor the nausea returned, and I ran to the toilet just in time.

Me: What the hell is going on? Do I have food poisoning because

I know I am not pregnant?. Or could I be pregnant?

I never had nausea when I was pregnant with my girls, so my

guess was maybe I had food poisoning. But everyone ate the

food, and I am the only one ill. I did not want to entertain the

ideal I might be pregnant so soon, but I needed to get to the root

of the problem and soon. I did not want to possibly get anyone

else sick if I was coming down with something. So, for kicks and

giggles I decided to get dressed and go purchase a pregnancy

test.

I returned to the house and immediately went towards the kitchen

to get a pickle. I needed something salty to deal with my

stomach. I really did not want or even feel like eating right then.

I took the box to the bathroom to take the test to eliminate the thought of me being pregnant. I did not have to force myself to pee on the stick. As soon as I sat down it was almost immediately, I peed all over the stick. After wiping it off I sat it on the counter and got in the shower hoping the warm water would help. By the time I get out I should have some results.

I got in the shower and was almost immediately comforted by the soothing warm water and steam from the shower. I could have fell asleep in there, but I knew that was not practical plus I had my pickle that seemed to help so I got out of the shower ready to start my day anew. I dried off immediately, got dressed and went to the kitchen to make a grocery list to go to the store. I wanted to make sure there was enough junk in the house for the weekend since I was not going anywhere and would be spending it with the family.

I got ready to grab my stuff to head out the door when suddenly I remembered the pregnancy test I had taken.

Me: Oh shit, the test.

I strolled back into my bathroom unbothered to read my results. I just knew I was not pregnant, but I just wanted to ease my mind before I headed out. I grabbed the box to read it so I would know what I was looking at. I picked up the test and immediately dropped my purse and keys.

OH BOY, OR GIRL!

As I stand here looking at the positive pregnancy test in my hand I just want to cry. On one hand I am happy to make my husband happy by expanding our family but how can I be too sure this was Kevin's baby. What if I was carrying Dre baby? There was no way for me to tell at this point. I know I needed to quickly make a doctor's appointment and possibly an appointment to terminate this pregnancy. I was terrified because terminating a pregnancy was the last thing I wanted to do. I had heard several horror stories about the process, and I really felt some type of way about killing a child. Maybe I could pull this off somehow and hopefully the baby would be my husbands? I should have broken it off with Dre several times, but I let my body control my reasoning. This was my regret stage, and I needed the support of my friends. I knew they were both just getting back in town, but I needed them, so I sent them a text to meet up.

Me: We need to meet up asap! I need some support right now in the worst way. Meet me at the Sandwich shop in fifteen minutes.

As I sat there waiting on my girls to reply to my text my nerves began to get the best of me, and I became extremely nauseous. I must have peed and threw up at the same time because my head was in the toilet and my panties were damp by the time, I heard my phone go off.

Keri: I will drop what I am doing and head that way girl.

Rae-Rae: Do I need to bring my gun with me because you know I am down to fuck someone up.

Me: No gun is needed unless it is to shoot myself. Just meet me at the shop asap and I will explain everything.

I went to quickly clean up and change my clothes so I could head out. Hiding this until the right time was going to be harder than I could imagine. I had never been this sick while pregnant with my girls which made me even more nervous. Could this be the boy that my husband wanted? How could I explain me being so nauseous all the time to Dre or my husband? At some point both would become suspicious.

Keri: I am heading out now honey.

Rae-Rae: Me too. I am ten minutes away.

I pulled myself together, threw the test into my purse and headed out to meet up with my friends. I was the first to arrive, so I quickly grabbed us a table and got me a sprite to settle my stomach. Soon Rae-Rae came walking in and joined me at the table.

Rae-Rae: What is going on girl? Are you ok?

Me: Girl life has just hit me head on and I do not know what to do.

Rae-Rae: Is it Kevin or Dre girl? I can handle both.

Before I could go any further Keri came through the door like a concerned parent. I could sense the I told you so coming from her.

Keri: Girl I did sixty to get here, what is going on?

Me: I am in a world wind of trouble right now and I needed someone to talk to.

Rae-Rae: Oh, shit is this some criminal type of shit?

Girl do we need to get some bail money together?

Keri: What girl you are scaring me right now?

I reached in my bag and pulled out the dreaded evidence and laid it on a napkin on the table. Rae-Rae: Oh shit!

Keri: Your pregnant! But that's good news, right?

Rae-Rae: Yeah, I thought Kevin wanted another baby?

Me: Kevin does want another baby, but I am not sure if this is his baby or Dre.

Keri: Girl you cannot be that stupid! Do not tell me you have been sleeping with Dre unprotected!

Me: Do not make me feel worse than I already do! I messed up, ok. I do not know what to do next. I want to make my husband happy with another baby but what if this baby isn't his, then what?

Rae-Rae: First you need to make an appointment to narrow down your conception date and to see how far along you are. Do you have any clue?

Me: My periods have never been regular so there is no telling. I pray I am only four weeks. But if I am further along there is a better chance of it being Dre baby.

Keri: Have you told Kevin anything yet?

Me: I have been so sick that I am not going to be able to hide it. I must tell him tonight.

Rae-Rae: Are you going to tell Dre?

Me: I have no idea how to even tell him. Hey Dre just wanted to let you know that I am pregnant, but I am not sure if the baby is yours or not. I do not think I can tell him.

Keri: You have too if there is a chance this is his child.

Rae-Rae: How about you just have an abortion and forget this shit

ever happened.

Keri: Abortion? Hell no! Why would she kill her child? It is not

the child's fault.

Me: I am not having an abortion. I am going to go to a clinic to

confirm the pregnancy and find out how far along I am then take

it from there.

Keri: That sounds smart.

Rae-Rae: I can go with you first thing in the morning. You know

we will be there for you every step of the way girl.

Keri: Yeah, we are here for you.

Me: Tomorrow is so soon, and I am terrified to even find out. I need to boss up and do this because this could possibly change my family for the worst. Ok, tomorrow morning it is.

Keri: I will meet you at the clinic as soon as I drop the kids off.

Rae-Rae: I will come pick you up in the morning because I know your nerves will be shot.

Me: Ok.

I did not have the strength to argue with my girls because they were right. I could not put this off too long. I needed to know so I could figure out my next move. I had never been so scared in my life as we all parted ways and I returned to my truck to head back home.

On my way back home, Dre texted me and said he wanted to see me this weekend. I almost ran into the back of a truck trying to respond to him.

Me: I do not know if this weekend is good for me.

Dre: Ok, well hopefully you can make a little time for me. I took off a few days because I was not feeling too good today.

Oh shit! He was sick just as I was. I could feel the urge coming back to throw up, so I quickly pulled over. After I relieved myself, I could not help but cry because I could remember being pregnant with my girls and Kevin having sympathy symptoms. At this point I was convinced that I was carrying Dre baby. I had to know what he was feeling.

Me: I am sorry you are not feeling well. What is wrong?

Dre: I guess I have a taste of food poisoning because I woke up throwing up. I did have Chinese food last night. Maybe it did not sit too well on my stomach.

Me: Yeah, maybe the Chinese food did it. Go lay down and I will try and talk to you some time tomorrow. I am spending the weekend with the family.

Dre: Ok babe cannot wait to see you and hold you. I know things have been crazy between us the past few weeks, but I want you to know that I miss you and I really do have some feelings for you.

I could not help it, but I wanted to throw my damn phone out the window but before I could the phone rang, and it was Kevin.

Me: Hey babe.

Kevin: I came home for lunch to surprise you, but you are not here. Is there something you want to tell me babe?

Me: What do you mean? I am headed home now. I met up with

the girls for a few today.

Kevin: So how are you feeling?

Me: I am feeling fine babe and why are you acting all weird?

Kevin: Oh no reason I will see you when you get here. I love you

so much.

Me: Ok, I love you too.

That was so weird that a knot came up in my stomach. My nerves

were working overtime knowing Kevin would be at the house

waiting on me. I looked and felt a hot mess and I knew this

pregnancy would not let me be great. How the hell can I keep

this from my husband long enough to settle things with Dre? I

just wanted to turn my truck around and completely disappear,

but I could not run from a situation I created.

Before long I was pulling in my driveway flustered and nauseated but trying to hold it together. I just wanted Kevin to leave and go back to work so I could figure some things out. I hoped he was not coming home for a lunch break quickie again. I just swallowed hard and placed a peppermint in my mouth and entered the house.

Me: Kevin, where are you?

Kevin:(yelling) In the bedroom.

Oh, hell no I could not handle a quickie right now! I just want to take a hot bath and lay down. My head was starting to swim as I walked towards the bedroom doors and I could feel myself becoming nauseated again.

Me: What is going on in here?

As I opened the doors to the bedroom, I could see Kevin sitting

on the edge of the bed smiling with a familiar box in his hand.

How could I be so fucking stupid! I was in such a hurry to meet

up with the girls that I left the box to the pregnancy test on the

counter. Shit! There was no hiding this shit now. He just

happened to come home to surprise me and got a surprise

himself. I was horrified.

Kevin:(smiling) So, where is it? Are we pregnant or what?

I just wanted to disappear inside of myself and never come out at

this point. I did not know what to say to my husband, but I knew

I had to say something.

Me: Well, I took the test this morning and it was positive, but I

have not seen a doctor or made an appointment yet.

Kevin: Hell yeah! I did that baby girl. We are going to have a baby! I am so in love with you right now. Do you need anything? How are you feeling?

Kevin was so damn happy I could not do anything but cry because I knew the possibility of this not being his child. He thought I was crying because I was happy, but it was the opposite. I was horrified. I did not want this to turn out bad. I wanted this to be his baby because anything else would possibly destroy my family.

Me: I am a little nauseous, but I am ok. I have pickles in there and they seem to help with the nausea.

Kevin: You did not have that when you were pregnant with the girls. Sounds like a boy to me plus I am not feeling any different like before.

He jumped up and gave me a kiss and then proceeded to speak to

my belly like whoever in there could hear and understand him.

Kevin: Hello little baby this is your daddy, and I will never ever

leave your side. I cannot wait to see you for the first time and hold

you.

Me: You know the baby cannot hear you?

Kevin: Yeah, your right. I am just so excited. My beautiful wife is

carrying my seed, everything is perfect. I love you so much. I

must finish up my shift, but I will get the girls and be home soon.

Just relax today I do not want you to stress about anything.

Me: Ok, but first I want to soak in the tub.

Kevin: Ok babe I will see you soon.

Kevin planted a kiss on my forehead and headed out the door. As soon as I heard his car crank up, I dropped to my knees crying. What had I done and what the hell just happened? I knew I was in for some trouble but at this point I just did not know how much. There was no hiding it and regardless of the outcome of the conception date I would have to carry out this pregnancy because my husband knows, and he would never want an abortion. My life, my marriage and my kid's life were about to change. How did my life become so damn complicated suddenly? The life of a housewife could not get any worse, or could it?

Oh well, I guess I will soon find out.

SHAKY GROUND

Once Kevin left the house I was in a state of shock and mad at how careless I had been. Not only was I pregnant and did not know if my husband or side guy was the dad but on top of that my husband now knows and is excited. I prayed hard that this baby would turn out to be Kevin's baby and not Dre's child. Somewhere in the back of my mind I knew it was Dre baby and was already trying to figure out how to conceal this from both men. I like dying would be easier than dealing with this drama and for once in my life prayed that nature would do its thing and I would miscarriage.

I knew I had an appointment at the clinic in the morning and my girls would be there to support me, but I still felt like shit. I allowed myself to be a fool for a man outside of my marriage and look at the position it put me in. I was sitting here on the edge of my bed terrified. My husband wanted this baby so badly and now I was not sure I could even include him in this pregnancy until I found out exactly when I could have conceived. These thoughts made my head start back the swimming and before I knew it, I was back in the bathroom throwing the fuck up.

Once I pulled myself together, I sent out an SOS text message to my friends.

Me: Y'all would never guess what happened when I got home. Kevin was here and he found the pregnancy test box I accidentally left lying around. I am dead!

Keri: Holy shit! What did he say?

Rae-Rae: Well, we know he was happy.

Me: He was extremely excited, but I could not bring myself to come clean to him about it possibly not being his child. What the fuck am I going to do?

I thought I had more time to figure this shit out. On top of that Dre texted me on my way home and told me he has been feeling sick and throwing up all day.

Keri: That is not good. My husband had my symptoms when I was pregnant with my son.

Rae-Rae: Wow is all I can say, bitch. Let us just see what the outcome is in the morning when you see a doctor.

Keri: Yeah, maybe it is just a coincidence that Dre is sick right now. It does not necessarily mean anything.

Me: I really do hope so. I seriously do not want to see or talk to him right now either. He was trying to see me this weekend, but I told him I would be busy with my family so that gives me a few days with him. All I can do at this point is prepare for the worst and hope for the best.

Keri: Well regardless of the outcome we are here for you.

Rae-Rae: I will be there first thing in the morning to get you. You do not need to drive now,

Me: This is just too much. Dre was not even worth all this drama.

The sex was the best I had ever had but, in that moment, I meant what I said about him. I was a mother first and this could possibly alter my children's life. I honestly did not want to leave my husband and it was not because of the kids. I really did love him. I just needed more attention from him, and I got all I was missing in Dre.

Me: Ok let me try and pull myself together. I needed to go to the grocery store, but I do not think I can handle that right now so I am just going to soak in the tub and then prepare dinner for tonight. I know Kevin is going to come home a brand-new man.

Rae-Rae: Well, call me if you need anything.

Keri: Same for me I am just a phone call away girl.

Me: Thank you both.

I needed so badly to relax so I just got in the tub to soak and try to relieve some of the stress. I stayed in there until the water turned cold then got out and got dressed. I had to try and act normal, so I grabbed a pickle and my grocery list and headed out to the grocery store.

I returned home from the grocery store with an hour to spare before my family was expected home. It really did not leave much time to cook but I threw my best meal together, hell I bought half the store, so I had many options. While I waited for them to arrive, I dined on vanilla ice cream and Oreo cookies while watching Jerry Springer. Now normally I would have watched this junk, but I figured with all the drama on the show maybe I could seek out a bit of information or ways to conceal my secret. I would've opted for a soap opera but my favorite had gone off by now. The cookies and ice cream were hitting the spot and mellowed me out for a second. When I was pregnant with my girls it was always a part of my daily diet. But in the blink of an eye, I started to get sick all over again and raced to the bathroom to once again throw up. I was glad I was not employed

because this was enough alone to get me fired. This nausea thing

was so intense that it would cause me to cry before I was

finished purging myself. After rinsing my mouth out, I decided

that it was best I stuck with something salty and grabbed another

pickle and some salt and vinegar chips and plopped back on the

couch just as the chime on the front door went off. Just like

clockwork my family was back home.

Me: Hi babies, how was school?

Reign: It was good mom.

Raeleigh: Yeah, I had fun and even got two snacks.

Reign: Dad said we were having another baby.

Are we having another baby?

Holy shit Kevin! You could not keep quiet for even one damn day and now my babies know. I had to think fast and quick but say the right things.

Me: I do not know yet little women. Mommy must go to the doctor first. Your daddy is just so excited about having a child that maybe he is pregnant.

Raeleigh: That's funny momma. Daddies cannot have babies only mommies.

Reign: You guys are so weird. I have homework to do.

As Kevin entered the house, I shot him a look of disbelief and he knew he was in trouble.

Kevin: I am so sorry babe, I got excited when I saw their faces and it just came out.

Me: Kevin what if there is something wrong in this pregnancy and I end up losing this baby? Now is not the time to worry the kids with adult issues. I hope you have not told anyone else, have you?

Kevin: Honestly just my Sergeant, my mom and dad but that is all!

Me: KEVIN!

Kevin: I am sorry babe. I am so sorry I did not think about how you felt right then. I promise I will make it up to you. See I even brought my favorite girl flowers.

He could tell that I was beyond pissed and the fact that more people knew further complicated things.

Kevin:(laughing) So looks like you are having ice cream, cookies, pickles and chips for dinner?

Me: It is not funny, the dairy made me sick, but the salty stuff is helping.

Kevin:(whispering) Salty foods huh? That sounds like my boy!

Me: Shut up, you are on punishment. Now go in there and fix our daughters plates. Too much movement makes me nauseous also.

Kevin: As you wish my queen.

I just wanted to jump up and strangle that man. Instead, I just chose to relax and try not to think about it. Hopefully in the morning I would be getting some good news. Just then my phone went off and it was Rae-Rae calling me.

Me: Hey Girl.

Rae-Rae: So, have you killed Kevin yet? I know he is over there being all special and extra.

Me: Girl he had the nerve to tell his boss, his parents and our girls. You know I am pissed right now.

Rae-Rae: Hate to say it but yep that sound just like him. Well, your appointment is at nine in the morning so I hope you will have breakfast done when I get there. You know a sister will be starving.

Me: of course, when is your little ass not starving?

Rae-Rae: Girl do not hate the player. So, have you heard anything else from you know who?

Me: Hell no! and even if he called or texted, I would not answer or reply. I have too much on my mind right now and he is part of the problem.

Just then Kevin walked in the living room to hand me a plate and sit down to eat with me.

Me: Well girl he who shall not be named just served me my

dinner so I will see you in the morning.

Rae-Rae:(laughing) Ok. Tell motormouth I said, Jack ass!

Me: Kevin, Rae-Rae says Hello. Bye girl.

Rae-Rae: Bye.

Kevin: Why was Rae-Rae suddenly being nice to me?

Me: She was not I just translated it into something nice for you.

Plus, I told her what you did today.

Kevin: Babe, I told you I was sorry. To make it up to you how

about a massage tonight?

Kevin did have magical hands when it came to massages. It had

been so long since he had done this for me, and I felt I needed it.

Me: Sure, only if it comes with a foot rub.

Kevin: Ok, deal.

And just like that I was back in an ok mood but waiting for my massage. When the girls finished eating and getting their baths, we all chilled in the living room for a while. It was the weekend and we both would be home, so we kicked off our family weekend fun with a game of Uno and then watched a movie until the girls fell asleep on us. Kevin carried them to bed one by one while I grabbed a bag of chips and headed to our room. I was looking forward to my massage the whole time he was in the shower but I guess my body had other things in mind because I never received the massage. By the time Kevin

got out of the shower I was sound asleep, so he climbed in bed to catch up with me.

IS THERE A DOCTOR IN THE HOUSE?

The next morning my nerves were so bad thinking about going to

the clinic that I burned the bacon.

Reign: Mom are you ok? You have never ever burnt bacon before.

Raeleigh: Yeah, my bacon is too crunchy.

Kevin: Do you want me to finish breakfast babe?

My mind was on the doctor's visit and not on cooking at that

time. Plus, the smell of bacon and eggs made me want to throw

the fuck up so I had to take Kevin offer to finish cooking.

Me: Yes please. The smell of food is making me sick.

I went to the bathroom to once again throw up when I heard the

chime on the front door. The only person it could have been was

Rae-Rae. She promised me that she would come get me to take me to the appointment. So, I pulled it together to walk out to greet her as if nothing were wrong. Me: Hey there Bitch!

Rae-Rae: Bitch you look like shit on a stick now where is my to go plate?

Me: I had to stop cooking because I was getting nauseous plus I burnt the bacon.

Rae-Rae: Crispy bacon? No bitch I will pass on breakfast. So, are you ready to roll?

In my mind I was not ready to go because I did not want to face facts, but I could not put this shit off.

I knew sooner or later Kevin was going to want to go to a doctor's appointment so I needed to know information before letting him tag along.

Me: Girl this is not going to get any easier so let us roll.

We walked towards the kitchen where everyone was eating, and I gave my girls a hug and kissed Kevin and told them I would be back after a while.

Reign: Have fun mom.

Raeleigh: Bye mom.

Kevin: Do not worry about the girl's babe we have made plans to hit the pool. See you when you get back.

Rae-Rae: And all y'all act like I am not standing here, huh? No bye Auntie Rae?

Raeleigh: Bye Tee Tee Rae!

Reign: Your funny, bye Tee Rae.

Rae-Rae: At least my god daughters have sense to speak. As for

you Mr. have fun choking on your crispy bacon.

Kevin: Good to see you leave too.

Kevin and Rae-Rae have always been at each other's throats.

They were like siblings when they were in the same room. I

could not do nothing but shake my head and walk out the door

behind her.

Rae-Rae: Your husband makes my whole ass itch. But anyway, let

us go so we will not be late.

Me: Yeah, let us get this shit over with I am past ready.

Rae-Rae: What is that plastic bag for?

Me: Shit in case I feel the need to throw up.

Rae-Rae: Oh, fuck no! Not in my damn Land Rover you will not.

Bitch you better stick your head out the window like a dog.

Me: Bitch shut up and drive.

The way Rae-Rae drive we made it there in less than ten minutes

and I soon found myself signing in and sitting in the waiting

room. Luckily, it was not crowded but the few eyes there I felt

like they were staring at me like they knew I had done wrong.

Me: What if I decided to have an abortion would you be upset?

Rae-Rae: I would not but I am sure Kevin and Mrs.

Holy Keri would be pissed. But this is your choice and your life girl.

You must do what is right for you and your family.

Me: Yeah, your right.

It seemed as if we were sitting there for hours waiting on my name to be called. I was starting to think that Keri was not going to make it. Within minutes she came rushing in like she was late.

Keri: Girl, traffic by my house is a bitch.

What did I miss?

Rae-Rae: You missed her signing in that is all.

Keri: Ok good. How are you feeling this morning?

Me: I feel like I should be hung from a limb and beaten with a branch. I feel defeated already and I do not even know why.

Keri: It will get better darling, we are here for you.

Just then my name was called to come to the back and suddenly, I felt the urge to pee. Luckily, enough peeing in a cup was my first order of business then off into a room I went to check my blood pressure and weight. Both were good considering the stress I was under. Afterwards we followed the lady into a room that had a bunch of baby pictures, a uterus and an ultrasound machine.

Me: This room alone makes me feel worse. I am not sure I even want to see this baby.

Keri: Do not start that here.

Rae-Rae: She has the right to not want to see the baby. Under the circumstances I totally understand her thought process. This could possibly be Dre baby.

Why did she have to say the name Dre because at that moment I received a text from him saying, just thinking about you. I just sat the phone back down. I felt like if I responded or talked to him, he would just suck me back into him.

Dr. Waltz: Hello, how are you ladies doing? My name is Dr. Waltz. Which one of you is my patient?

Me: I am, and these are my friends. It is ok to talk in front of them.

Dr. Waltz: As you please. Well, we did a urine test, and you are pregnant but because of your cycles you are unsure of conception. Well, we will try to answer that today. Since we do not know about how far along you are, we will use the ultrasound machine to determine and then set you up another appointment as a follow up. Any questions?

Me: Not really.

Dr. Waltz: Good. I am going to step out for a minute so you can undress from the waist down and peep out when you are ready for me to come back in.

The doctor stepped out and I did as he asked, and Keri peeped out to let him know I was ready. It had been so long for me that I forgot about the wand ultrasound so I wasn't prepared for an object to be inserted into my damn vagina.

Dr. Waltz: Ok now there is the uterus and the ovaries. Everything looks good so far. Let me move around to see if your far along enough to get a good. Oops there you go hiding. There is your baby.

I wanted to cry but when I looked over at Keri she was already crying, and Rae-Rae was sitting there shaking her head.

Me: The baby looks rather big.

Dr. Waltz: Yes, indeed let me try and take some measurements.

Oh wow! Congratulation's mom! You are having twins!

Rae-Rae: What the fuck? I mean are you sure?

Keri: Oh my God!

Me: Twins! That cannot be twins do not run in our family!

Dr: Waltz: I am sure. Look here they are in two different sacs. So, you are pregnant with fraternal twins and they are measuring in at almost eight weeks. Congratulations! Would you like pictures?

Holy shit almost eight weeks! I was further along than I could have imagined. I knew for sure these were not my husband's kids. That was during the time Dre and I first hooked up. My husband and I were barely around each other because he was working so much. I just laid there in a state of shock and could not say a bitch ass word. This was bad, really bad. Not only was I pregnant but a bitch was pregnant with twins.

WTF!

Keri: Yeah, we will take a few pictures.

Me: No!

Rae-Rae: Are you sure about that?

Me: I mean no we only need one picture.

Dr. Waltz: Ok, there you go mom. We will schedule to see you

back in a month to check on the babies.

Me: Thank you.

As I got dressed and exited the room, I could feel my knees

buckle and I fell back on Keri.

Keri: Damn girl are you ok?

Me: No, I have to throw up!

I took off straight to the restroom and threw up before exiting the office. I was a nervous wreck and was thinking about having an abortion at that moment.

Me: I do not think I can do this. I cannot keep this lie up. I have to say something to them both.

Rae-Rae: Are you crazy or something? Do you want to possibly lose your husband?

Me: No, I do not but I cannot have him thinking these are his kids.

Keri: Well technically one could be his since they are fraternal.

Me: That's not good enough, Keri.

Keri: Yeah, your right. I am sorry.

Me: I am really considering having an abortion.

I cannot do this to my family.

Rae-Rae: Do you want me to take you home or what?

Me: No. I need to meet up with Dre. I must tell him. I know for a fact these are his kids. I was not having sex with my husband during that window of time.

Keri: Think about this before doing it. You are going to tell him before you tell your husband?

Me: I have to. He has the right to know.

Rae-Rae: Ok, we support you girl but I for one think this is crazy as hell.

Keri: I second that shit.

I knew it was a bold move, but I could not go through this by myself. This could possibly break up my family and I needed to know how Dre felt about this situation. It was not like he did not know I was married and we both knew what we were getting into. I needed to know if I was about to become a single mother. So, I picked up my phone to text Dre back.

Me: I am glad you texted me Dre because we really need to talk. I do not want to do this over the phone so I was wondering if it would be ok if I came by for a minute?

I did not know if he was at home, work or out somewhere but I knew I needed to have a serious conversation with him, so I waited for a response. I knew I could not take this sonogram home because Kevin would get upset, I went to a doctor without him. It would be easier to hide one versus several.

It seemed like Dre would never text me back, so we walked down the street to the park to have a seat.

Me: I am so scared. I feel like I am living in a nightmare right now. This cannot be real.

Keri: Girl you are carrying a heavy burden right now.

Rae-Rae: As much as I hate to say it, the truth will eventually hit the surface, so I guess it is better to come clean.

Me: That is what I am afraid of. That is why I want to go ahead and tell them both. But I must talk to Dre first. Afterall he is the father.

Just then Dre responded to my text that he was not at home right then, but he could be there in twenty minutes if I really needed him. So, I responded back to him immediately.

Me: I will see you then.

I knew I had to do this alone and having my girls with me would

seem as if we were ganging up on him and I did not want it to

seem like that.

Me: Take me home so I can get my car. He has agreed to meet up

with me in twenty minutes.

Rae-Rae: Are you sure you want to do this alone?

Me: Yes, I am.

Keri: I think that is a bad ideal.

Me: I do not want it to seem like we are ganging up on this man. I

will do this alone. I must face my own shit alone this time with

both men.

Rae-Rae: Ok, Girl. Call us when all this is over.

Keri: Yes, please call and let us know you are ok.

Just like that I was back in Rae-Rae car and headed home to jump into my car and head to Dre house. I had to move in stealth mode around my house once we pulled in because I did not want them to know I was back.

Rae-Rae: Be careful girl.

Me: I will.

With those words I slowly backed out of my driveway and headed to Dre house.

IN DOUBLE TROUBLE

As I pulled into Dre driveway, I could feel a knot in my stomach slowly rising and I became nauseous again. Luckily, I carry an emergency bag in the car for when I feel like I might throw up. After I took a pause for my cause I quickly threw a piece of gum in my mouth and proceeded to his front door not knowing what I would say. I was really hoping that he would not be there or maybe in the house with another woman. But I was not so lucky because as I rang the doorbell, I could hear him inside.

Dre: Hi there beautiful. Come on in.

Me: Hi Dre.

Dre: Do I get a hug? I have not seen you in almost two weeks.

Me: Dre I really do not think that is a good ideal.

Dre: Oh because I was sick? Well, you do not have to worry about that it was obviously food poison. I am good now babe.

Me: Dre I am not here for that. I really need to talk to you. Can I sit down?

Dre: Yeah, have a seat this sounds serious. Is everything ok?

I really did not know how or what to say to him and I was afraid of his reaction. But I knew the best way to say it was not to beat around the bush and just come out a say it. So that is what I did.

Me: Dre, I am pregnant.

Dre:(laughing) Girl quit playing and come over here and give me a hug and kiss.

Me: I am serious Dre. I AM PREGNANT!

Dre: Am I the father?

Me: Of course, you are. Why would I be over here saying anything to you. This is hard enough for me. I took a pregnancy test yesterday and my husband found it. He has no reason to believe that it is not his baby.

Dre: Oh shit! I am going to really be a father.

Me: Yes. I went and had an ultrasound done today so I brought it for you.

He had no idea what he was looking at, so I had to help him out. When he finally figured it out his mouth dropped, and he stood up and walked towards me. I thought he was going to hit me or choke me. But instead, he grabbed me and pulled me close and hugged me.

Dre: We are having twins! We are having two babies.

Me:(crying) Yes, I am pregnant with twins and I do not know what I am going to do. I was thinking about having an abortion.

Dre: Abortion? Hell No! Why would you do something like that? Look if you are afraid of your husband, do not be. I will help you raise these babies.

Me: Are you crazy? Did you not hear me? My husband believes he is the father. My husband! I am not your woman. I am married and I cannot let this ruin my family. I have two girls to think about also. I was hoping you would be ok with me having an abortion because of my situation.

Dre: I do not care about your husband, but I do care about you. I don't have any kids, so I care about these babies your carrying. And if they are truly my kids I want to be in their lives.

Me: I do not believe you. You are only thinking about you!

Dre: I will take care of you, your girls and these babies. I really do care about you Rhia. Do not kill our babies. I love you. Just leave him if he does not accept this and come be with me. Marry me, Rhia.

What the fuck just happened? I mean really what just happened here? This man was pushing me to the edge to a point where I could slap him and then he just says, marry me? I am living in the twilight zone. Did he say that he loves me? A part of me really did believe him because he has never given me a reason not to. But the other part of me was thinking about my husband and how he would feel about me throwing our marriage away.

Me: Are you fucking serious?

Dre: Let me do that for you. Let me be that man for you.

Would you believe at that moment he stepped in and kissed me so softly? And in that moment, I was smitten and weak by his spoken words. Maybe I was looking at this all wrong. I wanted for so long for my husband to give me the love and affection that Dre showed me. I tried hard to resist Dre touch, but I couldn't fight it and before I knew it we were on his couch naked and he was kissing me so tenderly between my legs.

Dre: I want you for myself, Rhia. I want you babe. Let me have you.

He felt so good that I forgot all about our current situation and gave into him. Before I knew it my body took over and I uttered the words.

Me: You can have me, Dre.

Those spoken words alone opened flood gates and Dre began to eat me like he never did before. It was like he was trying to taste my soul. And when he climbed on top of me, he did it in the most romantic and gentle way possible. He still handled me quite well delivering slow strokes as he kissed me softly. I was lost in the motion of his stroke and wet as a river. I was glad he had leather couches because we would have left a few stains. As he rose my body on top of him, I let out a sweet sigh and rode him while he caressed and sucked my breast. We both reached our climax at the same time and we just laid there looking into each other's eyes.

Dre: Just move in with me. I will take care of you.

It was a sweet gesture, but I did not see how that was going to happen. I was in love with two men, and I was torn. This pregnancy was a curse but both men saw it as a blessing and only one knew the whole truth. In that moment I remembered my family was home waiting for me.

Me: Oh, shit I got to go!

Dre: Do you want me to go with you to help you tell him?

Me: Are you trying to get shot? My husband is a police officer! No. I will try and call you when I get free.

Dre: Do not let me down, Rhia. I want to do this for you, babe.

I quickly got up and ran to the bathroom to clean up and put on my clothes. As I ran out the door I started crying. I could not believe what I allowed to happen. The girls were right. I should have never come over here by myself. I was in more trouble now than I was before I got here. Dre wanted to be with me as a family, but I already had a family.

The drive home was nerve wrecking and agonizing to say the least. I was flattered by Dre response but could not help but have a little fear of what the outcome could be. I knew I needed to tell my husband before he heard it from someone else. Dre sounded so adamant about being with me that maybe he would try and confront my husband. I wanted to call my friends so bad but I already felt the guilt and didn't need more guilt laid on me so thick.

I pulled in my driveway and could hear my kids in the backyard in the pool as planned. I tried to play it cool as I entered the backyard but as I watched my husband and my girls play in the pool, I became sad and started crying. I had to figure out a way to come clean to my husband.

Raeleigh: Mom is home!

Reign: Get in with us mom. Dad is the shark, and we are fish.

Me: I will just let me put on my swimming suit babies.

I walked in the house and changed into my swimming suit and as I went to exit the house my husband came in.

Kevin: Are you ok babe? I was getting worried you were gone so long.

Me: I am ok honey. I just had a little business I had to take care of, but I promise the rest of the weekend is for you three.

Kevin: Business? What business?

Me: I promise we will talk about it but for now let us just spend time with the girls.

Luckily enough he did not ask any more questions as we headed out the back door to the girls. We stayed in the pool for what seemed like hours until the girls got hungry and wanted pizza.

We ordered pizzas and played board games until the pizzas

arrived. I really didn't want the pizza because I was scared it

would make me sick all over again so I just picked the salty

pepperoni off and ate it.

Raeleigh was the first to tap out as usual so Kevin put her in the

bed and Reign went to her room to watch movies until she fell

asleep. As for me I went to run some bath water because I

needed the jets from the tub to ease the stress from the day I had.

Kevin followed me to the room as usual with his hands behind

his back.

Kevin: I got something for you, close your eyes.

Kevin was not a man of many surprises, so I wondered what he

had in store. I closed my eyes anyway and when prompted to

open them Kevin was standing in front of me with a box in his hand.

Kevin: I know we have an anniversary coming up and we will celebrate ten years of marriage, but I felt now was the best time to upgrade your ring. You have sacrificed your body once again to give me another precious gift and I just wanted to show you how much I appreciate you.

When he opened the box there was the most beautiful wedding ring I had ever seen before. I know it cost a grip by the size of the diamond.

Me: Oh my God Kevin you did not have to do this.

But I love it.

Kevin: I love you more.

Me: So, do I still get that massage you promised me yesterday?

Kevin: You can have whatever you want. You are carrying my seed.

And just like that the moment was ruined for me but I did not let him see it. I just went and got in the tub and Kevin eventually followed me and joined me. Once we got out the tub, he made good on my massage. I enjoyed it thoroughly, but my mind was occupied by how to break the news to my husband, I knew I had to do it but I needed to choose the right time and soon.

The next morning, I tried several times to have the serious talk with my husband, but it never really seemed to be a good time. The girls were all over us and we never really got any time alone. I had to figure something out and soon because Dre continued to text me to let me know he was thinking about me and he loved me. In a strange way I was thinking about him also, but I loved my husband. I did not have any free time to text him back to talk to him, but I did text my friends, I had not let them know what happened the day before and to be honest I was scared to tell them.

I invited the girls over and of course they came. Keri brought her husband and kids so they could swim with my kids. Her husband

and my husband got along surprisingly good and would sit up

and have drinks and cigars whenever they were together. So,

Keri family was a good distraction to my family so I could get

the girls together to give them the piping hot tea.

The guys were inside in our lounge area having scotch and cigars

and the kids were content in the pool, so the girls and I settled on

the patio in the shade with a pitcher of lemonade.

Keri: So, what happened yesterday?

Me: I went over there with every intention of setting him straight

and cutting ties and somehow, we ended up having sex.

Keri: Are you serious?

Rae-Rae: Damn he must have a dick of gold! How the fuck do

you keep falling for his bullshit?

Me: This man told me he loved me, he wanted to marry me, and he was willing to help me raise my kids and these babies. He was excited about me being pregnant. He was against the abortion suggestion. He even offered to help me tell Kevin what was going on. He does not want another man raising or even thinking these are his kids. On top of that I have not even mentioned I am having twins to Kevin.

Keri: Damn well I commend him for wanting to do the right thing, but he cannot expect you to leave your husband.

Rae-Rae: I am just saying, so how good is the dick really?

Keri: Focus.

Rae-Rae: Sorry I am back. So, when are you going to talk to Kevin about it?

Me: I have tried all morning that is why I called you two nuts over.

Keri: Wait what is that on your hand?

Rae-Rae: Are you wearing another man's ring?

Me: Kevin gave it to me last night as an early anniversary present.

Rae-Rae: I do not see Kevin letting you go without a fight. Hell, I see Dre fighting for you. Must be nice to have two men fighting for your love.

Keri: This is not the ideal situation.

Me: I know I care for them both, but I truly do not want to break my family up. My girls would be devastated.

I already felt bad and surprisingly enough my friends were laying the guilt trip on me. They were quite understanding, even motherly Keri. I just wished I had a crystal ball so that I could see how all of this was to play out.

Keri: Where is the sonogram?

Me: I gave it to Dre. I could not risk bringing it in this house.

Rae-Rae: Well, that was smart of you because Kevin would have found it. You know you have an appointment in a month, so you have to say something.

Keri: Yeah, we cannot cover your ass forever.

I knew they were right, but I was so afraid of splitting up my family. What if Kevin could not forgive me and file for a divorce? What if he takes my girls from me during a divorce? I did not work so how would I be able to provide? All these things played in my head though I knew the right thing to do. Me wanting a little more out of my marriage turned into something much bigger that I was not prepared to deal with.

Keri: Look I know your scared. Maybe your kids can spend the night at my house and that would give you time and space to talk to your husband.

Me: That would be helpful because I do not want the kids around when we talk. Kevin has never raised a hand to me or ever been violet, but I do not know how he will react to me telling him I have cheated on him.

Rae-Rae: I wish that motherfucker would raise a hand to you! I am going to jail and hell in the same sentence!

Me: I do not believe he ever will.

Keri: You cannot say what he will or will not do until he does it. Same for Dre, what if he intentionally got you pregnant?

I never thought about that. What if he did get me pregnant on purpose to try and trap me and put me in this position. I began to get sad and angry all at once. I was once just a normal housewife living a normal but boring life. Then I got caught up in a romantic fantasy of an affair and now look at the mess I am in.

Me: I do not think Dre would do something like that. He seemed shocked by the pregnancy news.

Rae-Rae: Hell, that could have been an act.

Girl do not be gullible.

Just then Reign ran up to the table followed by the rest of the kiddie clan.

Reign: We are hungry and tired of swimming.

Can we go inside now?

Me: Go ahead.

Keri: My kids are always hungry. I will go in and fix them some

sandwiches.

Keri ushers the kids inside to fix them a meal and check on the

men children.

Rae-Rae: You know if things go sour tonight, you can always

pack a bag and come stay at my house for a while. At least until

you figure somethings out.

Me: Thanks girl but I am hoping my husband and I can work

through this. I do not think he would give up on this family so   .

easily.

Rae-Rae: I hope your right, but you can always call me no matter

what. Well fuck all this mushy shit girl let me get my ass home. I really do not have much to do but after the week I have had at work alcohol is calling my name.

Me: You are crazy. Thanks for coming by and I will call you if I need you.

After Rae-Rae left I decided to check my phone and I notice that Dre had called and texted me. I figured now was the best time to see what he wanted since Kevin and the girls were occupied. I know it was a bold move but I couldn't have him constantly calling and texting even though I kept my phone on silent. So, I decided to follow behind Rae-Rae and call him.

Dre: Hello?

Me: Yes Dre.

Dre: I was just wondering if you were ok.

Me: Yes, I am fine. I told you I would be spending the weekend with my family and I would call you if I could.

Dre: Well, I was just wondering how did your husband take the news and had you given anything I said any thought?

Me: First off, I have not had the opportunity to talk to him and secondly, I have not given our conversation too much thought. I have enough going on right now and could really use a little space from you. You are a distraction right now and I do not need that.

Dre: A distraction? I was not a distraction when you were laid up in my bed getting dicked down. I was not a distraction when I was giving you what your husband was not. but now that you are carrying my seeds, I am a distraction.

Me: Look I did not mean it like that just give me a couple of days to process this is all I am trying to say. I will contact you soon. Bye!

I was not going to hold no long ass conversation with Dre, and I hope he did not expect me too. I needed to get back in the house to my family and friends but not before reading Dre text message he sent after I hung up.

Dre: That is how you do me? Just hurry up and tell that nigga wassup so we can be a family.

Dre was losing his mind if he thought I was willingly leaving my husband to be a happy family with him. That is what I get for my pussy being too damn good.

I headed back into my house as my girls came running up hugging me with an overnight bag in tow.

Reign: See you tomorrow mom.

Raeleigh: We are going to Tee Tee Keri house.

Keri: Hope you do not mind I told them you said it was ok and they ran for some clothes.

Me: Girl you have no ideal. Thanks, because I feel like tonight is the night.

Keri: Oh really?

Me: I have no choice. Someone is losing their damn mind.

Keri knew exactly what I meant by that and ushered her husband to head towards the door. Keri: Well, we will see you tomorrow some time. Just give me a call when you are ready for the kids to come home.

Me: OK.

Girls: Bye daddy!

Kevin: Bye angels.

Once the house was empty, I started getting nervous and

nauseous again, so I went to the kitchen to get a pickle and sit

down.

Kevin: So, we have the house to ourselves. What shall we do

first? Movies, dinner or maybe both?

Me: Kevin how about we sit down and talk.

Now I do not know what it is about a man when you say you

want to talk but Kevin gave me a look like he lost his best friend.

My chest began to hurt every time I opened my mouth to start a

conversation, so Kevin began the conversation.

Kevin: I can tell something has been bothering you since you found out you were pregnant. But I assure you that you do not have to worry we can handle another baby. Everything will be ok, and we can still take our planned family vacation. I promise you nothing will change.

Me: But Kevin that is it everything will change. Nothing will ever be the same between our family.

Kevin: How is that? The girls will come around to having another sibling. Is it that you do not want this baby?

Me: Kevin I really have to tell you something.

Kevin: Whatever it is baby I swear we will work it out.

Me; Kevin, I am pregnant with twins and…

Kevin: TWINS! Baby I love you so much. Were you worried I would be upset or something?

Me: That is not all.

Kevin: What is going on?

Me: I am sorry baby, but I cheated on you and I truly do not believe these babies are yours.

I DESERVED THAT

I had never in my life seen Kevin so pissed off. He stormed out

the house without hearing another word and had not returned. It

was morning time, and I was sitting at the counter with a glass of

orange juice waiting on Kevin to walk through the door. I was

devastated and wanted to explain myself to my husband. I tried

calling him a few times, but he never answered. I texted my

friends to let them know what happened the night before and

Rae-Rae assured me she was coming over. Keri had my girls, so

she was not coming by until later. I did not want my girls to see

me like this. The nausea was starting to become manageable but

now depression was creeping up on me. I had no one to talk to other than my friends. I could not call Dre because he would complicate things more with his words.

It was not long before Rae-Rae showed up with two breakfast sandwiches, Oreos and coffee. An odd combination but I told her to pick up the Oreos for me.

Rae-Rae: Has he called or texted you back yet?

Me: No, he is still ignoring me, and he is not at Keri house. I do not know too many of his friends number. I am starting to get worried Rae-Rae.

Rae-Rae: He probably just went to a hotel to blow off a little steam. I am sure he will call or come home soon; he loves you.

Me: I hope so because I do not know what to tell my girls when they come home. I just cannot believe he stormed out without even letting me explain. The minute I said that he possibly was not the father of my twins he got up and just walked out.

Rae-Rae: Damn, and you told him you were carrying twins?

Yeah, that was a double blow to him. His pride is hurt, and he just needs a minute to get it together. But you know he loves his girls and would not stay away too long. Right now he knows they are not home so he's going to stay gone.

Me: I cannot really blame him. I just want the opportunity to explain and to let him know I am sorry, and I really do love him. I do not know what he is thinking and that scares me.

I am a stay-at-home mom I don't work so what if he leaves me? I have not had a damn job since college girl. What the fuck am I going to do?

Rae-Rae: Kevin is not going to leave you. You are going to the extreme now. Just give him some space and some time.

I did not want to give my husband any time to dwell on this without an explanation. A man's imagination can make him bat shit crazy when it comes to his woman. I know the thought of someone else fucking me was playing over and over in his mind and I did not want that. I needed to figure out where he was and talk to him.

I tried to remain calm but then my phone started going off. It was not Kevin instead it was Dre. Dre was the last person I wanted to hear from right then. I wanted to smooth things out with my husband not Dre.

Dre: How are you today beautiful?

Me: Today is not the day.

Dre: What? So, I cannot call to check on you and my babies?

Me: Dre I talked to my husband last night and things did not go too well. I am not in too good of a mood right now.

Dre: Well, I am glad you finally told him, but I am sorry your upset. How about I take you to lunch to take your mind off things for a while?

Me: Dre I have no idea where my husband is and how would it look if he sees us out? I am still a married woman. I made a mistake once and I am not going to continue to dig myself in a deeper hole.

Dre: Mistake? Once? Babe we have been together several times and you cannot say you do not feel something for me?

Me: Dre that is not fair!

Dre: Look I am sorry I know your hurting. How about you come

over and I fix you some lunch?

Me: I am not leaving my house right now. I have my friend here

to comfort me.

Dre: Well, if you change your mind all you have to do is call me. I

told you I want to be there for you and my babies.

Me: I hear you Dre just give me a little space to figure things out,

please.

Dre: Ok. I will be thinking about you beautiful.

Call me if you need me.

I was so glad to get him off the phone. Rae-Rae sat near me

burning a hole in me the entire conversation. She did not like that

he felt so comfortable to just call or text me whenever. He started off something on the side and somewhere along the way things

shifted. Maybe it was because of me being pregnant.

Rae-Rae: He is doing the fucking most. Me: He is just

concerned.

Rae-Rae: Concerned about splitting your marriage up and

stepping in.

Me: Please do not start I am worried enough. I just cannot believe

that he has not called or text me. He is really upset with me.

Rae-Rae: If the shoe were on the other foot you would react the

same way.

She was right I would be pissed if my husband cheated and had

children on the side. I had always prided myself on being

married to the father of my children. I felt that gave me a leg up

from most women and now look at me. Here I am now a statistic and having to fight for my marriage. I was just hoping and

praying that he is not thinking of getting a divorce.

Rae-Rae: There is no sense of sitting in this house feeling sorry

for yourself. Why don't we get out for a while and get you some

fresh air?

Me: I do not want to be out right now, but we can hit the patio. I

just wish I could have a drink right now.

Rae-Rae: How about I make margaritas and I will just make yours

a virgin and add whip cream?

Me: Sounds like a plan to my black ass. Extra whip cream on

mines!

Rae-Rae was like a professional bartender when it came to drinks

and I could not pass that up even though mines would not

include alcohol.

While on the patio waiting on my drink, I texted Keri and tried to call my husband again. He did not answer the phone, but he finally did text me back.

Kevin: I am where I am trying to process our conversation. I just cannot believe you would do me like that.

I could tell in his text that he was extremely hurt. I did not want to hurt him, but I did not want to continue to lie to him. I just wanted to come clean about my dirt.

Me: Baby, please come home so I can explain everything to you. I do not want any more lies or secrets between us plus what am I going to tell the girls when they get home?

Kevin: Tell them that their mom is a slut that cheated on their dad.

Me: Kevin that is not fair, I am still your wife and the mother of your children.

Kevin: Are you my wife? A wife would not do no hoe shit like that. Then you fucked some random nigga raw, lay up in my bed and have the nerve to get pregnant. There should never be a possibility that I am not the father.

NEVER!

Me: I understand that I did wrong in our marriage, but we are not talking divorce, are we? I love you and want to be with you. I am willing to come clean.

Kevin: Right now, I do not know. I do not know if I could look at you the same. I will be home tonight but only for my girls, not for you.

Me: Ok. That is fair but give me a chance to explain myself, please.

Kevin must had enough because he did not text me back but the fact he said he was coming home was just enough for me. Keri text me also to tell me she was coming in an hour with my girls. I must pull myself together so my girls won't be affected and see their mother in distress. I also had to figure out a way to tell them that I was pregnant. I figured I would wait until Kevin and I was on better terms. Then there is Dre, I just do not know what to do about him. He treats me good, the dick is immaculate, and he wants to be with me all the way. Dre dick stayed on my mind. Even now I feel like I am cheating on Kevin because the thought of Dre between my legs makes me wet as fuck.

Rae-Rae: Your over here in la-la land. Did you get some good news or something?

Me: Well Kevin finally text me back and he will be coming home tonight.

Rae-Rae: That's good news, right?

Me: Yes, but on the other hand I cannot get Dre out of my head. Even now I want to go to him.

Rae-Rae: Damn, the dick is that good huh? Is he better than Kevin?

Now I really did not want to answer that but the look on my face told it all. I could not hide it.

Me: I have only been with two guys in my life and Dre listens to my body and gives it exactly what it wants. With Kevin we are just having sex and going through the motions. My body misses him and needs him.

Rae-Rae: Damn girl you got it bad honestly.

Me: I honestly cannot be around him and not want to wrap my mouth around his dick. I am getting turned on now just thinking about him. Why did I have to get pregnant? I had my cake and was eating it too.

Rae-Rae: I am your friend and I want to see you happy. Who do you honestly want to be with?

My body screamed Dre, my mind screamed Kevin and my heart was torn between the two. I was starting to feel like the only reason I wanted to stay with my husband was because I was financially secure and because of my girls.

Me: I do not really know.

Rae-Rae: Bitch, you know who you want. Just be real with yourself. Speak that shit and go after what you want.

Rae-Rae made a lot of sense and I needed to be honest with myself. I deserved to be happy one hundred percent or not at all. If I stay with Kevin, there is a possibility that I will never hear the end of my mistake. If I decided to be with Dre, I could lose more than I gain. I had to make that phone call to let him know that I choose him and just deal with the consequences.

Me: Your right. I have made my decision and I am going to call him to let him know I choose him.

Rae-Rae: Him? Kevin or Dre? Who are you talking about?

Rae-Rae asked who as I walked in the house to make my phone call. I was going to need a little privacy to deal with this situation. I was about to fight for what I wanted, and I knew I was going to have a fight. But I believed that my kids deserved to see their mother happy no matter what. And I deserve to be with someone who will deeply appreciate me and respect me the

way I wanted to be respected. The more I thought about it as I

held my phone my mind, body and soul all were on one accord

and I knew I had to dial the number.

Me: Hello, are you busy? Can I please get a moment to speak

without any interruptions?

POURING OUT MY HEART

Me: Is that ok with you?

There was nothing but silence on the other end of the phone, but I could hear him breathing so I knew he could hear me. It was now or never to por out my heart to this man and hope that he would still be in love with me. I already knew there was a chance I could lose both Kevin and Dre, but I did not want to end up alone. So instead of one of them determining my future I decided to take it in my own hands and make the first move. I was tired of hoping things would work itself out and work in my favor. I did wrong and it was time I owned up to it.

Me: I really do care for you and I know you still care for me. I know I have been a little distant with you lately, but I needed time to think and sort things out. I love my girls and I do not want them to be a part of a broken home. I want my girls to have a mom and dad to raise them as a family together and I have always believed that was the correct way to raise a family. I have prided myself on having both of my children having the same father and never wished to have children outside of my marriage. But here I am. And it hurts me to separate my family. But I have realized that my children will benefit more from a loving blended family just the same. What I am trying to say is Dre I want to make this work with you.

There it was. I finally poured my heart out to Dre which is something he has wanted for a while and it felt good to let him know how I felt.

Dre: Babe I could not be happier with your decision.

I promise I will treat you like a queen and your girls like my own. I just wanted the chance to possibly show you that I can be what you are looking for all in one man. I may be younger but baby I swear I can handle this, and I got you.

Me: Thank you. That means a lot to hear you say that. I am sure my girls will respect you and learn to love you as well. I am just so scared of making this major shift in our lives and how my girls will react.

Dre: That is why you need to be strong so they can feed off your energy. You got this and I am one phone call away if you need me. Have you spoken to your husband yet?

Me: He will be home later as will my girls. I will talk to him first.

Dre: I love you girl! At any time if you are afraid to be there pack a bag and come directly to me. I got you.

Me: Thanks, I will let you know what happened later ok?

Dre: Ok, Babe.

As I hung up the phone, I strolled back outside to face Rae-Rae
and her Hennessey and Coke.

Rae-Rae: Sooooo Bitch?

Me: What?

Rae-Rae: I will choke a pregnant bitch!

Me: I called Dre and talked to him.

Rae-Rae: And!

Me: I let him know that I wanted to be with him, and I just wanted
to make sure he was ready for what is to come.

Rae-Rae: I knew it! I knew it! You have not been genuinely happy for years with Kevin. Since Dre has been in the picture you have been a lively bitch like in college. Girl go with your gut. I support you and I am happy if you are genuinely happy.

Me: I am, and I am excited to see where this goes and then with two new babies. I am just worried that Kevin will not let this end peacefully.

Rae-Rae: Well, you know how men are and mommy Keri might not be as happy. You know she was hoping you drop Dre off the face of the earth and make it work with Kevin.

Me: Yeah, I know. She should be here soon, and I wish I could have just one drink.

Rae-Rae: Well, you know I will not tell. You can have a sip of my drink. I imagine one drink will not hurt.

As bad as I wanted that drink and to take Rae Rae up on her offer I declined. But she was right I would have to deal with Keri side eyeing me once I tell her my decision. I really was not looking forward to telling her or Kevin to be honest. But I was not going to have time to practice my speech because I could hear car doors close, and I knew it was Keri.

Reign: Hi mom, did you miss us?

Me: Yes Baby.

Raeleigh: Hi mommy. I had so much fun. I want to show daddy my picture I colored for him.

Me: Daddy is not home right now babies. Why do not you two go inside and play for a minute while I talk to your Tee Tee.

Girls: Ok!

Here goes nothing. Rae-Rae was gulping her drink and grinning because she knew what was coming.

Keri: So, what has the goon squad been up too?

Rae-Rae: Oh, I have been chilling and drinking all day. Had to babysit our girl for a minute.

Keri: So, I take it you told him and he didn't take it too well judging by the fact he isn't here.

Me: Yeah, he stormed out and up until an hour ago he was not answering my phone calls. I told him I cheated and that I was pregnant with twins that were not his.

Keri: Oh wow! We will let him blow off a little steam, he will come home and you two can start to heal.

Rae-Rae and I just kind of looked at each other. We both knew

she was not going to like what I had to say next.

Me: Actually, Keri I am not interested in making things work out

relationship wise with Kevin any longer. I feel I have not been

happy for years and I deserve that.

Keri: Are you insane? So, your telling me you're going to throw

your marriage away? Am I the only one who takes marriage

seriously? Tell me your joking? Rae-Rae she is joking right?

Me: No, I am not joking.

Keri: What about your girls? Did you stop to think about how they

would feel?

Me: I have been my girls and they will be better off in a

household filled with love and happiness.

I did not want to sound like an Al Green song but hey that is how it rolled off my tongue.

Keri: So, let me guess, your choosing to create this happy family with Dre? This is a joke! As your friend I will support you but that does not mean I agree with your choice. I must go. I promised my husband I would just drop the girls off.

I could feel the steam coming from Keri as she gave me a hug and exited the backyard. Welp that did not go too bad. That was good practice for my conversation with Kevin.

Rae-Rae: Well, I guess you are on punishment with momma Keri! She is hot at your ass. But this is your life, and you only get one.

Me: Yeah, she is upset as fuck, but she will get over it. I must live my truth. I know it will be hard for a minute, but I have faith I made the right decision for me and my children. You know how

Kevin is! He is not going to want me to keep these babies because he is not going to want to raise another man's children. I will hear about this shit damn near every time he looks at these babies. I cannot live like that.

Rae-Rae: Yeah, that would suck to have to walk on eggshells daily in your own home. Then he probably will not trust you out of his sight.

Me: My point exactly and I cannot live that life.

Rae-Rae: Well, you do not have to wait too long to have a conversation with Kevin because I see lights pulling in your driveway.

My heart sank and I could feel myself getting nauseous. I turned just as the headlights went off and a door slammed. I knew it was Kevin, who else would it be? I was ready but I was not ready all at the same time. All I could do was take a sip of water and

prepare for this rollercoaster of emotions as Kevin walked

through the gate.

Kevin: Rae-Rae.

Rae-Rae: Kevin.

Me: Kevin can we talk for a minute out here? The girls are in the

house and I do not want to alarm them.

Kevin: Let me go in and speak with my girls while you get rid of

your company.

Kevin stormed in the door as Rae-Rae, and I just blinked at each

other.

Rae-Rae: Your company? Girl let me get the fuck out of here before I say something stupid and end up locked up tonight. Call me if you need me.

Me: Ok and thank you again for being so supportive.

I felt so fucked up as Rae-Rae left. I felt a lot safer with her here but it was apparent that he didn't want her here. Maybe he was blaming my friends too. You know hoes of a feather flock together. I just wanted to say fuck it and pack a bag and just go to Dre house. I could not leave like this though. I had to make sure Kevin knew what I had decided regarding these babies and our marriage. I just swallowed all my fears and walked in the house to check on my girls. Kevin was in the kitchen warming them up something to eat, laughing and talking as if I had not said shit to him. I guess we were going to play that game. Well, he can play that game by himself. I patiently waited on him to give the girls their food before I said anything to him.

Me: Kevin can I please speak with you outside?

Kevin: Can that not wait?

Me: Do you really want to pick a fight with me in front of the girls?

Kevin stormed out to the back patio as I stole a pickle from Raeleigh plate. I could tell he only came home because of the girls and he could give a damn if I was here. I could basically pack a bag and go stay with Dre and he would not give two shits if his girls were home. I could tell he did not care what I did at this point and that made my decision easier, and I knew I made the right choice. We were still married, in the same house and he could not look at me or talk to me. Fuck him too.

Me: So, is this what we are doing now? Are we in middle school or something, Kevin?

Kevin: You cheated on me so what the fuck do you want me to say?

Me: I simply asked you if we could have a conversation like two adults. We have children, Kevin. Or have you forgot that?

Kevin: Are you fucking serious? You seemed to forget that when you were fucking some other man.

Me: Kevin look I am sorry first off. I never meant to hurt you honestly. Things between us have not been too good for the past three or four years. All you do is work and we never spend time together and I honestly got lonely.

Kevin: Lonely, huh? Get a fucking puppy, a job, a fucking hobby Rhia and not a fuck buddy! Is this someone I know?

Me: Not that I am aware of.

Kevin: How long has this shit been going on?

I really did not want to answer that question, but I knew honesty was going to be best.

Me: we have been seeing each other for about three months.

Kevin: Oh damn, so I am working hard for my family, putting my life on the line and my wife has a whole fucking relationship. You better hope I do not know this motherfucker.

I could tell Kevin was pissed but was trying his best not to get emotional.

Kevin: You are not keeping this fuckers babies. I want you to set an appointment to terminate asap. I refuse to live with this constant reminder of your infidelity.

Me: I cannot do that, and you know that. Kevin: So, your saying your keeping these babies?

Me: Yes.

Kevin: Well, there is nothing left to say then. I guess the next step would be a divorce and you can go and be your fuck buddy pregnant whore.

Me: Really? Now your just saying shit to hurt me. I am still the mother of your children!

Kevin: Oh yeah and speaking of children if you think your taking my girls away from me your crazy. The girls will stay with me. You can pack your shit and leave.

Me: Are you crazy? So, we are not even going to be reasonable adults about this?

Kevin: Bitch you do not work, your pregnant with some other man's kids and you think I am going to allow my girls around some man I do not know. Yeah, your fucking crazy. You fucked this marriage up and you want to walk away like nothing happened? Why are you even here? Why don't you just go be with your babies daddy?

Me: I want us to still be decent for the sake of the girls. We still need to be parents to raise our girls and us constantly at each other's throats is not going to help our girls. I was hoping we could work this out ourselves. You know be cordial with one another. I'm not trying to take the girls from you but you want to take them from me and that's not fair to them.

Kevin: No what is not fair is their mother is a whore. Now you are more than welcome to go be with your boy toy. You need to quietly go pack your shit and leave my house.

Kevin was extremely mad but I didn't want to make a scene

because the girls were there and through it all I was pregnant. I

will admit I did feel guilty but from our conversation I knew I

made the right choice. Things between us would never be the

same. I went back into the house and sat with my girls for a

while to tell them I would be gone for a while but would see

them soon.

Reign: Momma is everything ok?

Me: No baby but I promise your momma and daddy loves you

both, ok?

Raeleigh: Are you going on a mommy vacation?

Me: Something like that baby. No matter where I am, I am still

your mother and I love you both.

I can see tears in my girls eyes and that hurt me so I couldn't do anything but walk away. I didn't want to pull them from their home when I really didn't know where I was going so I left them with their dad. I packed me a bag, hugged my girls and headed to my car. Once in my car I called Dre to see if I could stay at his house and of course he told me to come on. I texted Rae-Rae to tell her what happened and to let her know I would be at Dre house.

Of course, when I pulled into Dre's driveway, he was sitting

outside waiting for me. I got out the car in a state of shock and

ran straight into his arms. He hugged me tightly and assured me

that he would never abuse my heart. In this moment I thought

back to the first time we met and I looked at Dre as a player or a

play toy. Here was this man standing here comforting me after

my husband put me down and belittled me. It was like Dre was

my Prince Charming in this moment. He placed the sweetest kiss

on my forehead, grabbed my bag and walked me into the house.

Once inside he took my bag to his bedroom and came back out

and sat next to me. I was still beside myself and just playing

everything back in my mind. My life just did a complete circle in less than twenty-four hours. It was just too much to handle and I began to cry.

Dre: Baby, please do not cry. You are safe now and I promise I will do all that I can to help you through this tough time. I stand by my word and will take care of you and our babies.

Dre: Are you hungry cause I can fix you something or go get you something?

I wanted so badly to open my mouth and say something or show my appreciation but my emotions were erratic and I couldn't stop crying.

I knew I had a long battle ahead of me with Kevin and some healing to do with my girls.

Dre: Baby, please talk to me. Just tell me what is going on in your mind.

Me: I have never been treated so badly before. This man just threw me out of our home in front of my girls and they were crying. He called me a bitch, a whore and some more choice words. I do not think we will have a peaceful divorce. Hell I don't think he will let me keep my car. I am just assed out and do not know what to do.

Dre: I promise you that you are not alone and I will take care of this mess. We didn't plan this but life has a way of playing out for the better. You are giving me something that I never thought I would have.

Me: What is that?

Dre: I have always wanted children but was never fortunate to be blessed with them. Now look at you. You walked into my life in my time of loneliness like I did for you. We were both missing

something in our lives and we both filled that void.

Dre was right. It was like we found each other by chance. He

could've turned out to be some player or piss poor ass baby

daddy but he wasn't. he was willing to step up in a major way.

And we had a connection to each other like no other.

Me; Thank you so much.

Dre: You do not have to thank me. I'm just doing what any good

man would do for someone he cares deeply about. I told you Rhia

I love you and I meant that.

With every word he spoke I felt it to my core just like Kevin's

harsh spoken words. But Dre's words eased my pain.

Dre: Are you hungry?

Me: Not really, I am tired and have a headache.

Dre: Can you take Tylenol? I need to go buy a pregnancy book tomorrow so I can have some knowledge of what to expect.

Me:(laughing) Yes, I can have Tylenol.

Dre: Ok why don't you go to the room and get comfortable and I'll bring you a Tylenol?

Me: That sounds good. I want to take a bath first and then I will lay down.

Dre: Sounds good. I will run you some water while you unpack your stuff.

We headed into the bedroom and I unpacked as Dre ran me some water. I started feeling sad at the thought of having to start all over. I was just thankful that Dre was so understanding and took his part in the drama with grace.

Dre: Do you want bubbles in your bath?

Bubbles? That was so cute that I had to repeat it in my head.

Me: Yes, please.

The days event had worn me out and all I wanted to do was get

in the tub and relax and then lay down. I proceeded to get out of

my shoes and clothes as Dre came around the corner. He walked

over to me and kissed my lips, my stomach and then led me to

the tub. I thought he was going to get in with me by the way he

was looking at me.

Instead, he sat behind my head and gave me a Tylenol and a

glass of water.

Dre: Is the water too hot?

Me: No, it is perfect, thank you.

Dre took the glass of water and began messaging my temples. Never in my life had I been pampered and catered to like this. Kevin always thought the fact that he brought home a check was good enough. But he always forgot about me, my wants and my needs. Here Dre was treating me like a queen. I just laid my head back in his lap and let him work his magic.

I must have dozed off because I woke as Dre was stepping into the shower behind me. I watched his silhouette for a minute in the shower before deciding to join him. Him and I have had some good times in that shower before and with the way I was feeling I wanted to recreate those moments. I stepped into the shower with Dre and began to lather his back with soap. It was like a scene straight out of a movie or something. As soon as he turned around and gazed into my eyes, I fell into his body like I belonged there. He was more than ready as he grabbed me by the back of my head and kissed me. His touch was like no other as steam began to fog up the doors. He slowly ran his nails up and down my body before picking me up and placing my back against the wall. He knew exactly what I wanted as he slowly slid down my body until I was nested on his shoulders. He kissed my thighs and slowly lifted my body up until his lips were placed directly between my legs and he began to French kiss the hell out of my clit. I could not do much but grab his head as his tongue moved up and down between my lips. He was damn good at pleasing me and it didn't take long for me to climax but he wasn't satisfied and wanted more.

As my body trembled, he continued to please me and moved his tongue in and out of me while gripping my ass firmly. It was so sexy how he was concentrating and looking as he watched my body rise and fall with his soft strokes. I could feel my thighs tightening up around his neck so I grabbed his head and pulled

him in closer to make sure he didn't miss a drop. I could tell he

really liked that because he rose to his feet with a grin on his face

as he slid me down his chest.

Dre: Are you in the mood for me tonight?

It was so sexy how he said that shit. I felt like a school-girl

having sex for the first time. You would have thought that with

all I had to happen in the past twenty-four hours that sex would

be the last thing on my mind. Well, you would have guessed

wrong because Dre had a way with me to make me forget about

things.

Me: I am always in the mood for you.

We both grinned at each other for a second and then he kissed

me on my neck as he slid me down on his dick. He felt so good sliding in me that I could not help but moan and bite my lip as he bounced me up and down on top of him.

The water hit so perfectly between us as it ran down our bodies washing the soap and all my stress away. This was how I imagined real passion. We soon switched positions as I bent over and grabbed my ankles for Dre. He loved how flexible I was and I enjoyed the many positions he loved putting me in. He closed my legs, grabbed my hips and pulled me into him until he was all the way inside of me once more. With each thrust I could feel my legs trembling, but I did not wish for him to stop. He was pleasing my body from the inside out as I screamed out in pleasure.

Me: Please, do not stop.

Dre: Am I hurting you babe?

Me: Do not worry about that just fuck me.

I could tell he was holding back the force because I was pregnant.

Men are funny like that thinking that they can hurt the baby.

Granted Dre was not an average guy in size I did my best to show

him I was ok. I began rocking back pushing my whole body into

him to show him I wanted more.

Dre: Damn, Rhia! Shit that feels good.

Me: Yeah, Yeah. Oh shit, Dre.

He grabbed me by the back of my neck with both hands and

began to drill the shit out of me. I wanted to let out a scream but

he had my neck gripped so tight all I could do was moan and

grunt. I knew he was fighting the urge as I gripped his dick with

my muscles. He could not do shit but release my neck and put his

hands above his head.

Dre: Damn that shit feel so damn good, FUCK.

I just keep bouncing on his dick and gripping him until I felt like he was ready to cum. Then I immediately dropped to my knees and quickly took him into my mouth and started sucking. This pushed him over the edge as he leaned back on the wall and grabbed the back of my head. I wanted him to fuck my face and he enjoyed it.

Dre: What are you doing to me?

That was all he could say as I started playing with his balls while trying my best to swallow him whole. He wanted so badly to enjoy his moment but he couldn't hold it and soon released himself down my throat.

Dre: FUCK.

I rose to my feet and let the water run down my face and body

and exited the shower as if I had just won the battle. He could

not do nothing but watch me.

Dre: You are a bad girl, Rhia.

Me: I know I am.

Dre finally managed to get out the shower and dry off but I was

already laid in the bed.

Dre: How are you feeling now? Are you relaxed now?

Me: Yes, I am, thanks.

Dre: I'll admit you got me in the end but I still had that ass from

the jump.

Me: I did not say this was a competition but yeah, I won.

Dre: Yeah, you are the champ tonight girl.

Dre jumped in the bed with me just as my phone went off. It was Rae-Rae texting me to see if I was ok.

Rae-Rae: How are you feeling girl?

Me: Girl I am feeling a lot better. I just wish I could tell my babies good night.

Rae-Rae: Do not worry about that. Your girls know you love them and their smarter than you think. I want you to just relax. I will speak with a partner in my office and get you a good lawyer. Things will work out in your favor. Just keep playing Kevin's game a little longer.

Me: I will girl. I really appreciate all your help and support.

Rae-Rae: Have you told Keri yet?

Me: No. I could not handle any more stress today.

Rae-Rae: Probably best, I will talk to you some time tomorrow.

Take care of yourself girl, Love you.

Me: Love you too.

After I laid my phone down Dre could tell something was on my

mind and became concerned.

Dre: Is everything ok? Who was that?

Me: That was one of my best friends just checking up on me.

Dre: Are you sure your ok?

Me: I just wish I could tell my girls good night that is all.

Dre: This is only temporary. Do not stress yourself because of his

ignorance. Remember your pregnant and I need you and my

babies healthy.

Dre was right I did not need to stress about my situation. My body was finally getting the hang of being pregnant again and I did not want to alter that. There was a lot I was going to need to adjust in the following days including speaking with a lawyer. So I decided to simply enjoy this moment and get some rest because tomorrow would be a new day.

The next morning I woke to flowers and breakfast in bed. Dre was standing over me with a huge smile on his face as if he had just hit the lottery.

Me: Why are you so happy this morning?

Dre: Well, I got to wake up next to the most beautiful woman in the world. I did not know what you had planned today or if you wanted me to take off to stay home with you.

Me: I will be ok Dre but I appreciate it. I do not want you to miss out on any money because of me.

Dre: The money isn't important, you and my babies are.

I could tell he was serious by the look on his face.

Me: What kind of pill is this?

Dre: I noticed you didn't unpack any prenatal vitamins so I ran out to pick you up some and some milk.

Me: That is sweet. With everything going on I never did go buy any. Thank you.

Dre: I told you I will take care of you. Well, if you don't need me I will go in for a while but if you need to leave for any reason, I left a key next to your phone with the alarm code.

Me: Ok. See you later?

Dre: You know you will.

I sat up in the bed to enjoy my breakfast and Dre gave me a kiss before he went up front and eventually left the house. I picked up my phone to look at the time, I wondered if I called Kevin would he answer and let me speak to the girls. If I was there I would be getting them ready for school right now. I didn't want to take the chance and ruin my mood so I decided to do as Rae-Rae suggested and play Kevin's game a little longer.

As I finished my breakfast and went to the kitchen to wash the dishes I realized there was someone I needed to reach out to. I still hadn't told Keri what went on but as my phone started to ring I knew I wouldn't get a chance. I rushed to my phone to see it was Rae-Rae.

Me: What's up girl?

Rae-Rae: You sound very chipper this morning.

Morning sex will do that to you.

Me: For your information you freak Dre is at work but he did fix

me breakfast before he left.

Rae-Rae: Are you sure he is at work or are you sitting on his face

right now?

Me: Shut up! What is it?

Rae-Rae: Oh yeah. I spoke to an attorney here in the office that

handles situations like yours and as a favor for me he has agreed

to represent you.

Me: Oh great! Who is he?

Rae-Rae: Vincent Polk Me:

Wait the hell a minute.

Rae-Rae: WHAT?

Me: Is this the same Vincent you slept with after the Christmas party last year?

Rae-Rae: Maybe.

Me: No wonder he agreed to do a favor for you. I hope you explained to him I do not work and cannot pay him much.

Rae-Rae: That is the reason why it is a favor.

This pussy has power girl!

Me: Oh wow! I don't need to know nor do I want that image in my head.

Rae-Rae: Whatever can you be at my office around two o'clock to meet up with him and start on your paperwork?

Me: I have nothing else to do so I guess so.

Rae-Rae: Ok girl see you then. Oh and don't forget to let Dre up for some air.

Me: Bitch bye.

My girl meant well but she was crazy as hell. After I got off the phone, I just walked around the house for a minute looking for something to do. For a bachelor he was neat, almost like a neat freak. I could not really find much to do but I wanted to feel useful with me staying there so I gathered the few clothes I saw and started some laundry. I wanted to give myself some time for when I knew Kevin would be at work and I could get more of my things out the house. There were things there that I really wanted but I did not know how I would get them out the house. I did not want to involve

Dre so I would have to get my girls to assist me. What was I going

to do in this house until my appointment with Rae-Rae side nigga?

I finally decided to just lay down and watch television until it was

time for me to head out.

WHERE THERE'S SMOKE THERE'S FIRE

I woke up with just enough time to run out the house and head

down to Rae-Rae office to meet the attorney. I hate driving

downtown because parking is a bitch. I didn't have time to drive

around searching for a free spot so I chose the closest parking

garage possible. With fifteen minutes to spare I arrived at Rae-

Rae office door, knocked and entered.

Rae-Rae: About time.

Me: Girl I dozed off in front of the television.

Rae-Rae: So you still haven't spoken to Keri, huh?

Me: No, why?

Rae-Rae: I received a phone call from her about you. Obviously your soon to be ex-husband called her to inform her that you have moved out.

Me: WHAT? Why do he think he can call my friend?

Rae-Rae: He can play the victim with her and not me. I knew he was not going to call me. She's pissed the hell off about you being at Dre house.

Me: Well she's going to need to get over the shit and help me get my stuff out.

Rae-Rae: You know I am down. We can ride out after your meeting.

Vincent: Hello ladies.

In walks this tall handsome man who introduced himself as Vincent Polk.

Rae-Rae: Vincent this is my friend I was telling you about earlier.

Vincent: Ok, Mrs. Flint you can follow me to my office. I have all your paperwork ready for you.

Me: You can call me Rhia.

I followed Vincent into his office and had a seat. This was not the way I wanted to spend my afternoon but I knew I had to beat Kevin when it came to this divorce. I started explaining the reason for a divorce as Vincent took notes. I know I wasn't saying anything he hadn't heard before because he immediately assured me I would be just fine.

Vincent: What do you want to walk away with?

Me: I simply want joint custody of my girls, my car and enough money to maintain. He has already put me out of our home and I'm ok with that.

Vincent: Well the house was purchased in the marriage so he can't make that decision. The house will have to be sold and split down the middle. I will ask for half assets as well of all financials. Do not worry I will have this filed and he will be served immediately.

Me: Thank you.

I sat in there for another thirty minutes going over and filling out paperwork until my fingers hurt but in the end it would be worth it. I finished up with him and returned to Rae-Rae office.

Rae-Rae: I spoke with Keri and she is going to meet us at the house to get your things so we better head that way. Did he take your keys?

Me: No I have my keys. There is not much I want out of there. We should be able to get it all between our three vehicles.

Rae-Rae: Sounds good. Let us head out. I hate Mondays in this

place.

We headed out to the place I use to call home to get some of my

things. The whole ride I dreaded having the conversation with

Keri. I know she is mad at me for not calling her and she cannot

understand why. I did not really feel like arguing with her and

Rae-Rae assured me she had my back.

As we pulled up at the house Keri was already there standing in

the driveway like someone's mother.

Keri: So you're really leaving your husband, huh? I for one would

like to say I think this is a stupid move and why didn't you call

me?

Me: Can we get in the house first before you start with the shit?

Rae-Rae: You wonder why she did not call you?

Listen to yourself.

I walked inside and immediately started packing the rest of my clothes and a few other items. Before I knew it we were loading up six suitcases and four nice sized boxes. I even packed a few of my girls things. We packed my car full and the rest fit nicely in Rae-Rae truck.

We were all tired and just wanted to sit down for a second and I knew Keri was going to start back up with the shit. We grabbed something to drink and locked the house up and went to sit on the back patio one last time.

Me: You guys this is really happening right now. The attorney suggested to be fair the house can be sold therefore we can both profit and move on. I remember when we first moved in this house. The patio and the kitchen were the main reason I picked

this house.

Rae-Rae: Yeah, we have had some good times here.

But out with the old and in with the new.

Keri: Yeah, this patio is my favorite and the pool is to die for.

Maybe when the house sales I can buy it.

Rae-Rae: Too soon bitch.

Me: Why would you say something like that?

This is hard enough for me.

Rae-Rae: Because she is an inconsiderate, Bitch.

Keri: I was just joking you two. I am sorry, Rhia.

Rae-Rae: No, you like the pool so much why do not you just take

a few of the plants and flowers around it. You know for memories

and all.

Keri: Can I, Rhia? I really like the Aloe plant over there.

Me: Whatever I do not care, Keri.

Rae-Rae: Come on I will even help you.

Keri: Thanks Rhia. Rae-Rae I do not need your help. Your trying

to be fucking funny.

Rae-Rae: No bitch I am not trying to be funny. Our friend is

sitting over here in pain and you want to take pieces of her life.

How about you take her bitch ass husband also. Keri: Shut up.

I could tell Keri had pissed Rae-Rae off by the way she was

talking and looking. As soon as Keri got up and headed towards the pool so did Rae-Rae. I knew no good would come out of that

but I wasn't going to interfere.

Rae-Rae: Which one?

Before Keri could even answer Rae-Rae pushed Keri into the

pool but not before snatching the wig from her head.

Keri: Are you fucking serious? That was so fucking childish!

Rae-Rae: No your fucking childish!

Me: Wait a minute you two.

Keri: You better get that bitch before I yank her ass.

Rae-Rae: Yank who? Bitch why do not you get your tired ass out

of that pool and run home to your two pumps and a pull ass

husband.

Keri: Fuck you!

Rae-Rae: No fuck you! Do not forget your old raggedy ass wig too, bitch!

Keri quickly grabbed her things and ran to her car soaking wet. I could not do shit but stand there. Honestly, Rae-Rae did exactly what I was thinking.

Me: Two pumps and a pull? What the fuck was that?

Rae-Rae: She once told me that is how her husband has sex. He gives her two pumps and then pulls out.

Me: Oh wow! I do not think I would tell anyone that shit. You know she is never going to forgive you for that shit, right?

Rae-Rae: I do not give a damn. She pissed me off and that was so inappropriate. Hell, I love that damn grill, but you do not see me loading it up in my truck.

Me: Yeah, that was too damn soon.

Rae-Rae: Exactly.

Me: We better straighten up and get the hell out of here before he comes home to see us here. I'm sure he will change the locks after today but I don't care.

We straightened the patio area back up the best we could and then loaded our ass up so she could follow me to Dre house. With all the chaos going on I forgot to text Dre to let him know I was bringing more stuff to his house.

Me: Dre I hate to bother you but my friend Rae Rae and I are on our way to your house. I went and got some more of my things. I hope that is, ok? If you are home, we will see you in a minute.

I was expecting Dre to still be at work, but he texted back fast to let me know he was home and would see us when we got there. I was a little nervous with Rae-Rae meeting Dre for the first time

but since she was so supportive, she was the better choice.

When we pulled in Dre was sitting in his garage waiting on us.

Looks like he was expecting me to show up with a bunch of stuff

because he had cleared out part of his garage.

Dre: Welcome home babe. How are you feeling today?

Me: Hi Dre, I am feeling ok today.

Dre: That is my girl. This must be your friend Rae-Rae?

Me: Oh yeah. Rae-Rae this is Dre, Dre this is my friend Rae-Rae.

Rae-Rae: Hello there. Nice to finally meet you even though it is

under these circumstances.

Dre: Well, any friend of Rhia is a friend of mines. What do I need

to unload?

Me: I have a bunch of suitcases and boxes that is all.

Dre: Well, you ladies can go in the house and relax while I unload the vehicles.

Me: Ok.

Rae-Rae and I went into the house and crashed out on the couch. I just wanted to relax instead of reflecting on the day events but Rae-Rae was still pissed.

Rae-Rae: Can you believe that bitch? Now tell me I was wrong.

Me: I do not want to think about that mess but no you were not wrong by far. She knew better than that. She is just mad at me for my choices and then not saying anything to her. Maybe she is mad that I called you instead of her.

Rae-Rae: I still do not understand why she would be talking to Kevin like she is not your friend. Honestly maybe she wants him. We all know that her husband ain't worth shit.

Me: I do not think Keri would do nothing like that. I just think she feels some type of way. I just cannot dwell on her feelings right now I have my own shit going on and it is serious. If she is truly my friend, then time will tell.

Rae-Rae: Girl the drama and the fuckery is real out here. If your happy that is all that matters. Let your lawyer handle Kevin's ass. Speaking of Vincent, he did text me that all the paperwork been filed and Kevin should be served in a day or so. Are you ready for this?

Me: I am ready to get to my new life with a clean slate. I am ready to be done with this marriage and be a part of my girls lives again.

He has alienated me from them because he is in his feelings about the situation and that is not fair.

I am only playing his game because I am pregnant and do not want to fight.

Rae-Rae: Well bitch I am not pregnant and I will go head up with him.

Me: No, I will fight him in court. I have an ace up my sleeves.

Dre stepped into the house taking boxes into the bedroom, so I followed him into the room. I just wanted him to wrap his big arms around me for comfort.

Dre: Are you ok babe?

Me: I just wanted a hug. I had a rough afternoon with another friend but on a good note I did speak with my lawyer who is speeding things along.

Dre: Well, I do not know the situation, but a friend would stand by you no matter what. If not, then you need to remove the negative from your life. Let me know how much you need for the lawyer.

Me: Yeah, Rae-Rae said the same thing in so many words. The lawyer situation was taken care of by Rae-Rae. He is someone she has had dealings with.

Dre: Oh wow. Seems like I will like her then.

Me: Yeah, she is cool.

We walked into the living room with Rae-Rae who was now watching television.

Dre: Are you hungry or would you like a drink, Rae-Rae?

Rae-Rae: I would love some Hennessey, or anything brown you have.

Me: Damn girl.

Dre: Ok I got a Hennessey drinker on my hands. We are going to be cool. Do you play dominoes and cards?

Rae-Rae:(laughing) Hell yeah! I am a regular homie just happen to have breast.

Dre: Ok ok. Rhia, have you shown your girl around yet?

Me: No, we did not get to all that. We just wanted a moment to breathe once we walked in.

Rae-Rae: She did not tell you I had to push a bitch in the pool earlier?

Dre: Huh? The friend?

Rae-Rae: Yeah, her name is Keri, and she is not so much a fan of yours.

Dre: That is ok once she gets to know me, she will change her mind. Why don't you look at the house while I whip something up with these drinks?

Rae-Rae: That is sweet my guy. Just one drink will do me good. I must head back to my side of town.

I took Rae-Rae on a quick tour of the house and to my surprise Dre had done some rearranging of the house. A bedroom that was once empty now had two daybeds in it set up for little girls. I was shocked but grateful at the same time. I liked that about Dre, he was an action man. He said things but he always backed them up with actions.

Rae-Rae: Damn, you two already fixed up a room for the girls?

Me: He must have done this while I was gone. I knew nothing about it.

Rae-Rae: This man really does care about you.

He is opening his home to you and your girls.

I think you made the right choice.

Me: Yeah, I do too.

I finished up the tour and we made our way back to the front of

the house to the lounge area where Dre was. He was sitting at the

bar with a glass in one hand and a sandwich in the other.

Dre: Did you girls enjoy the tour?

Me: Dre, you didn't have to but I love the room for the girls.

Dre: I did it to show you that I mean what I say. I love you and I

want to be there for you, your girls and our babies.

Rae-Rae: Well, I for one am sold on this home and your generosity. You seem like a real stand-up kind of guy. I just want my friend to be happy and she says that you make her happy.

Dre: Well, I will do everything in my power to keep her happy.

Me: I am happy Dre.

Dre: Good, I made you some tea and a sandwich and Rae-Rae here is your Hennessey. I made turkey and roasted chicken sandwiches so eat up.

We sat up for a minute and just talked and those two fools finished a bottle of Hennessey. Dre even joked about naming one of the babies Hennessey.

I finally ran Rae-Rae off about nine o'clock and Dre and I got settled into bed after a nice shower. I needed all the rest I could get so I could get up and unpack my old life.

Days turned into weeks and my court date was slowly

approaching. Kevin and I had been to mediation and I was finally

getting my girls on a regular basis. Surprisingly, they loved Dre

as much as I do, and Kevin hated that. I got to keep my car, child

support, spousal support all in exchange for him to stay in the

house. I had not heard much from Keri since her and Rae-Rae

got into it. She would call or text me every so often just to check

up with or meet up for lunch. Those two still were not seeing eye

to eye and no one was willing to apologize so our girls' weekend

had not happened in months.

Dre and I were happier than ever and were anxiously waiting in

the lobby for my doctor's appointment. Neither one of us could wait to see our babies and the progress they have made. I was a

little over twelve weeks and already in maternity clothes but Dre

found my belly sexy and that didn't stop our intimacy.

Dre: I cannot wait to see my babies and hear their heartbeats.

Me: I know I am excited too, but did you have to bring a

camcorder with you? That is so old school.

Dre: Do not hate I want to record this for memories babe. This is

all a first for me and I want to remember everything. This is all

surreal. Will they be able to tell us the sex of the babies?

Me: You are doing the most and I think it is way too early to tell.

But we should be able to get some good sonograph pictures today.

I wish Rae-Rae could have made it today. I want to make her the

God mom.

Dre: Yeah, I like her. She has some bite to her.

Nurse: Mrs. Flint you can come on back.

Dre and I headed to the back into our room and anxiously waited on the doctor. It does not matter how many kids you have your always nervous when it comes to a pregnancy. This pregnancy was unlike any I have had. It started off rough but by now things were calming down, but I felt as if I had gained a lot of weight. The scale had not changed much but my clothes told a different story.

Doctor: Mrs. Flint how are you feeling today?

Me: I am feeling a lot better.

Doctor: Is this dad?

Dre: Yes, I am.

Doctor: Great! Well, your weight looks good and your blood pressure is perfect. We will look and see how the pregnancy is progressing and if possible, we will order a few tests.

Me: Test for what?

Doctor: Well, you have fraternal twins so we like to stay ahead of any possible complications in the pregnancy. Nothing to be alarmed about at this point. We can also possibly tell the sex of the babies from the testing.

Dre: Oh really?

Doctor: But it is only if it is necessary. Ok, lay back for me mom. You will feel some cold gel on your stomach.

I was so ready to see my babies the gel did not bother me. Dre was glued to the monitor with camcorder in hand as the doctor showed us two healthy babies. They were already active and seemed to be kicking each other.

Doctor: As you can see, we have some highly active babies. Let us get the heartbeat on the monitor.

The sound of their heartbeats was music to my ears, I was so overwhelmed with emotions I could not help but start crying as Dre kissed my forehead.

Dre: I cannot believe I am looking at my babies right now. I know it is early, but can you tell if they are boys or girls?

Doctor: It is still early but I am sure we will be able to tell at the next visit. If they are as active as they are now, we should have no problem getting a good picture.

This made Dre incredibly happy. He was hoping for a boy and a girl. I did not care either way I just wanted healthy babies. The doctor handed Dre a bunch of ultrasound pictures.

Doctor: Ok, you can carefully sit up. Everything seems to be progressing good. Do you have any questions for me?

Me: No.

Dre: No, thank you doctor.

Doctor: Well since you do not have any questions, we will see you back in six weeks. Try to get rest whenever your body needs it, eat right and continue your prenatal vitamins.

Me: Ok, thank you.

We exited the room after I made my next appointment and we walked out to his truck. He hesitated before he cranked up the truck and I could feel him staring at me.

Me: What's wrong, babe?

Dre: Absolutely nothing, babe. For once in my life everything is almost perfect in my eyes. I was just sitting here thinking about our future together.

Me: Oh really. So how is our future looking in your eyes? Right now, I can see some Chinese food or Italian food in my future. I am starving right now.

Dre: I am serious, Rhia. I love you and I am already in love with our little family we have blended. I just need to know that you really love me and that you are all in.

Dre looked at me with tears in his eyes and I knew this was a serious conversation to him. I was taken back by his intensity and level of emotions this man was giving me.

Me: Dre, I do love you and appreciate you for adapting to this life change so quickly. You make me happy and make me feel a way that I have never felt before.

Dre: Good girl that is what I wanted to hear. I know you are going through it with the girl's father, but I want to bring these babies in the world the right way. I know we have barely known each other for a year but I feel like this is right and it fits.

Me: What are you saying, Dre?

Dre: I am saying I want us to get married once you finish all this court stuff. I understand your pregnant and it does not have to be anything big and extravagant unless that is what you want. I would marry you in the backyard, babe. I love you and I want to be with you forever.

Me: Are you serious, Dre? I mean are you sure you do not want to wait a while?

Dre: Rhia, do you love me?

Me: Yes, Dre you know I do.

Dre: Do you want to be with me and raise our family?

Me: Yes, I do.

Dre: Then Rhia will you do me the honor of being my wife?

TOO FUCKED UP TO TURN BACK NOW

What the fuck am I going to do now? My marriage is over and I'm in too deep with Dre. I have to be rational in my decision but I just can't bring myself to say the words. I've already fucked up my marriage and I'm not 100% sure that these babies are Dre kids.

Me: Dre, I don't know what to say. I mean I think I know what I want but I need some time. This is happening all too fast and my divorce isn't final. Its just a lot to deal with right now. I hope you understand. I know what my mind wants but I need to make sure my heart wants the same. I don't want to hurt you.

Dre: Rhia I love you and that isn't going to change. I want to do right by you and make you happy. You can't tell me that you aren't happy when we are together. I can feel it. I know things between us escalated quickly but it's fate. Let's go grab a bite to eat and head back to the house. I don't want to stress you out but I do want to make it clear where I stand with my feelings.

He was right and I was happy but still confused. With all I had going on I still had feelings for the man I built a family with and married. At one time we were happy and deeply in love. There was still a small part of me that was still wishing this was all just a nightmare. But it wasn't. This was my new life that was created out of loneliness and lust.

Me: My favorite Chinese food and a nice massage sounds like a plan but can you drop me off at the house? I really want to get comfortable right now and lay down.

Dre: Everything ok?

Me: Yeah just really tired and would love to put my feet up before they start to swell. I am ok so you don't have to worry. Just make sure that you get extra egg rolls and plenty of fortune cookies.

Dre: (Laughing) I will make sure to get everything to the queens liking.

Dre dropped me off at the house and I couldn't think of anything but calling my girls. I needed all the advice I could get at that moment. I already knew that I would be severely scorned by Keri who still believes I'm making the biggest mistake of my life. Rae-Rae is my most supportive friend but she never really cared for Kevin from the start and always thought he was a jerk. I really don't feel like the arguing and going back and forth with these bitches on the phone so I chose to just call Rae-Rae.

Rae-Rae: What's going on my favorite Bitch?

Me: Girl I am so confused right now. Dre asked me to marry him when we left our doctors appointment.

Rae-Rae: WHAT!! Girl what the hell did you say? Shit are you going to let the ink dry on your divorce papers first?

Me: I couldn't answer him. I need some time to think and get my head together. I still care about Kevin and hate all this happened the way it did.

Rae-Rae: Girl fuck Kevin and the horse he rides on. You deserve to be happy. This is just a hurdle that you will get over. What did Keri say?

Me: I haven't talked to her yet. Have you talked to her lately?

Rae-Rae: Hell naw! She has been ghost lately and oddly silent. You think her and that roach like husband are into it again? She normally goes radio silent when they are into it.

Me: (Laughing) I don't think they are into it but she has been very private lately. She didn't answer my call the last time I called her but she text back she was busy.

Rae-Rae: Do I need to come get you and we both roll up on her? I know this heifer should be home.

Me: No I'm going to wait on Dre to return with my Chinese food and just stay in the house and relax. I've had one hell of a day and just want a little peace.

Rae-Rae: Well shit I'm out riding so I will try and reach Mrs. Sourpuss.

Me: Be nice girl. If you talk to her just tell her to call me tomorrow. I am sure I will see you tomorrow.

Rae-Rae: You know I will be over there so make sure Dre has a plate reserved for me. That man know he can cook.

Me: Ok girl. I'll see you tomorrow.

I got into some comfortable clothes, cut on the TV and waited for Dre to come back with my food. As I curled up on the couch and got comfortable under my favorite blanket a text message came through my phone. It was a message from Rae-Rae saying that she just rode by Kevin's house being nosey and she was sending me a picture.

As I waited for the picture to come through Dre walked through the door with my food so the drama Rae-Rae had could wait for a hot second.

Dre: Ready to eat babe?

Me: Hell yeah! The kids and I are starving for food and some attention. (Phone Flashes)

I sat my plate down as Dre walked back into the kitchen for

something to drink.

Me: What type of drama have this girl captured now? If anyone

can sniff out drama it would be Rae-Rae. (Looking at my phone)

Me: WHAT THE HELL? (Drops the phone)

Dre: What's wrong babe?

Me: Rae-Rae just sent me a picture. She's at Kevin's house and

Keri's car is in the damn driveway.

Dre: Why would your friend be at his house anyway? Did y'all

have a fight?

Me: I don't know what she's doing there but I'm sure Rae-Rae

will find out.